One of These Wylder Nights

by

Roni Denholtz

Wylder West Series

One of These Wylder Nights

Cover Art by *Tina Lynn Stout*

The Wild Rose Press, Inc.
PO Box 708
Adams Basin, NY 14410-0708
Visit us at www.thewildrosepress.com

Publishing History
First Edition, 2023
Trade Paperback ISBN 978-1-5092-4835-3
Digital ISBN 978-1-5092-4834-6

Wylder West Series
Published in the United States of America

"Tell me," she asked. "Where else have you watched the sun go down?"

"Arizona, California, New Mexico and Mexico, Kansas and, of course, Nebraska."

"Nebraska?" She watched his face as he answered.

"It's where I'm from." He made a slight grimace, but she caught the expression. There was something about Nebraska he didn't like. He leaned closer. "But these are the most beautiful sunsets."

Her blood was racing at his nearness. "Especially when they're shared," she murmured.

"Yes."

He bent his head towards her, and she tilted hers up. They hadn't had a chance to kiss last night—now—

He brushed his lips against hers. They were soft.

Almost instinctively, her hands went to his shoulders. He brushed his lips against hers again, and this time, her lips clung to his. Their kiss turned fiery in a second, and she was reveling in his strong shoulders, as his lips met hers again and again.

"Betsey," he murmured. She clung to his shoulders; the cloth of his shirt smooth beneath her fingers. She could feel the warmth of his body through the light fabric.

Praise for Roni Denholtz

"Roni Denholtz's ENCHANTED VERMONT NIGHTS is a delightful read!"

~*M. Kate Quinn, award-winning author*

Dedication

To My Aunt
Irma Paitchel Kulakoff
With Love

Acknowledgement

To my readers—

I have always been intrigued by tales of lost treasures, especially that of the legendary "Dutchman's Mine." The mine, supposedly discovered by a German man (Dutchman coming from those who speak Deutsch, or German) was supposedly a secret guarded by the Apache Indians. It was rumored to hold a fabulous amount of gold. The "Dutchman" closely guarded the secret, and to this day no one has found it, though many have searched the area of the Superstition Mountains in Arizona, where it is purported to be located.

I had the idea to do a story about a fictional variation of the mine, and created my Spaniard's Mine. I had a lot of fun setting the mine in the area of Wylder, Wyoming, the fictional town created by the editors of The Wild Rose Press. My husband and I visited the area 7 years ago on a trip to see Yellowstone National Park and to visit the wonderful western museums in Cheyenne.

So my fictional treasure trove came to life and, since I had been considering a story for Betsey, cousin of my hero Drew Covington of "One of these Nights" I started thinking. Would characters searching for the mine try to reach the deceased Spaniard via a séance to learn the location of the mine? Instantly, I saw a need for Betsey in the story, and the character of Vaughn sprang to life too.

I hope you enjoy my version of the famous legend and get a chance to visit the beautiful state of Wyoming, a truly amazing place!

Roni Denholtz

Chapter 1

Betsey Chalmers alighted from the carriage, glancing around for the man who was supposed to meet her. Who among the people near the stagecoach was he? Her stomach tightened as she scanned the group.

Dry heat met her skin. The West was certainly different from New York City's humid spring season. She could even see the dust swirling in the street.

Behind her, Nina, her lady's maid, stepped down.

She wasn't sure what the man looked like. She was supposed to meet either her cousin Drew's brother-in-law, Joe, or his business partner, Vaughn. They had described Joe as a man with dark hair and blue eyes.

She was finally in Wylder at last, but which man was he?

Betsey's eyes caught sight of the nearby telegraph office. Fine. She could telegraph her cousins that she'd arrived safely in Wylder, Wyoming, as soon as she met her escort.

"Miz Chalmers?"

Betsey turned. A dark-haired man sauntered up to her.

He was tall and clean-shaven. His shoulders were broad in his blue shirt and tan vest. He was good looking, the kind of man who would immediately get a woman's attention. Dashing—and just a little disreputable looking, with his lean face, dark eyes, and almost suspicious expression.

Her heart fluttered in a most unexpected manner. "Yes?"

"I'm Vaughn Montgomery, Joseph Moore's business partner." He stuck out his hand.

She shook it. She'd already observed that out here in the West, people were less formal about introductions. "A pleasure to meet you, Mr. Montgomery."

"Vaughn," he corrected, "will do."

Nina gave a stiff and proper curtsey.

"This is Nina Smith, who has accompanied me," Betsey introduced her. "All right, Vaughn," she agreed. She glanced around. "Is Joseph here, too?"

"He's back in the cabinet shop," Vaughn said, tilting his head down the street, "talking to a customer about a special order. He asked me to come and meet you. We have a room reserved for you at the Vincent Hotel." He included Nina in his glance.

"Here are the lady's bags," the coachman announced as he and the man riding shotgun moved things off the top of the stagecoach to the wooden boardwalk.

Vaughn Montgomery leaned down and lifted Betsey's case. He then picked up Nina's smaller one. Both women grabbed the carpet bags they'd also brought along. They'd be here for several weeks.

"This way," Vaughn instructed.

Betsey and Nina hurried after him, striving to keep up with his long strides. "I have to send my cousins a telegraph telling them we arrived safely."

He turned to regard her. "I was going to do that as soon as I get you settled in the hotel."

"Thank you." They followed him to the hotel, walking down a street and around a corner. Betsey's skirts swished against the wooden boardwalk. The dust that people and horses stirred up in the town was more prevalent than she'd expected, and she could actually see particles floating in the air. Still, the air was incredibly clean compared to New York City. She took in a deep, satisfying breath. The sky was an intense blue, with few clouds, and a fresh smell unlike the smells of the city where she'd grown up and lived.

Of course, out in the country, where her cousins resided, the air was clean, too. But it seemed like the western sky blazed even more brightly.

They passed small stores such as a milliner's shop and a gun shop where several cowboys stood looking in the window. She observed a fairly large mercantile displaying boots and a candle-maker's as they walked towards the hotel.

They entered the Vincent Hotel. It was nicely furnished, with plush seating and small tables scattered in the spacious lobby, and appeared clean. One elderly gentleman sat in a chair reading a newspaper and smoking a pipe. The scent of tobacco reached her.

She drew a sigh of relief. Her mama would have wanted her to stay at a clean place. Thoughts of her Mama made her momentarily sad, and her steps slowed. It had been less than a year since she'd lost her.

"If you'd like to freshen up after you check in," Vaughn said, "We can meet you at the restaurant here." He pointed to the adjoining room, where the clatter of dishes met her ears. "Joe will meet us there in thirty minutes. Will that suffice?"

"Yes, thank you," she murmured. It was late

afternoon, and she was used to eating later meals in New York, but she knew she'd have to adapt to different ways in the West.

"I'll telegraph your family." He tipped his hat and left.

She signed the register. "Joseph Moore paid for your first week," the clerk, a man with gray hair, declared. "Says you're a cousin."

Nina signed in, also, after a quick look around.

"Yes," Betsey agreed. A cousin by marriage, actually; but it was better for women traveling by themselves to be thought of as having relatives nearby to look after their welfare. So they had agreed she was to say Joseph was her cousin. Her family had insisted she bring Nina along as extra protection, although her meek maid was not in favor of this trip.

A young man took their belongings. They followed the clerk up the stairs and down a corridor to Room 16.

The room was spacious and neat, with a parlor and a bedroom with two beds, and she breathed a sigh of relief. The clerk pointed out the shared water closet in the hall, and then left them to unpack, freshen up, and get settled.

She was not sure how long she would be at this particular hotel. Her plans with Joseph had not been firm. They had agreed she'd stay at the hotel for at least a week. After that, she and Nina might stay with Joseph, or even out camping with him and Vaughn in the Medicine Bow Mountains.

The unique job she'd come out here to do was going to be a challenge, especially without her cousin Drew and his wife Violet to help. But Violet was expecting their first child in about a month, and Drew did not want her traveling or having the baby in the "Wilds of America." She smiled at the expression. That's what their Cousin Patricia called Wyoming, even though it had become a state in 1890.

After washing up and unpacking a few items, Betsey went to the window and looked out.

Wylder, a town not too far from Cheyenne, appeared to be a bustling town. The *clip-clop* of horses rang out clearly. People chattered as they strode up and down the street. Wylder did not appear anywhere as big or busy as New York City, of course. But it appeared to be just as large as Twin Bridges, in New Jersey, where her cousins resided.

The May sunshine of late afternoon slanted across the street, casting the other side in deep purple shadows. She had seen some mountains at a distance out the window of the stagecoach as they approached and wondered if those were the mountains which held the mine that they sought.

What mysteries were hidden there? Was the Spaniard's Mine truly located there?

The Spaniard's Mine. It was legendary, the stuff tales were spun around. There were so many rumors that it seemed there must be *some* basis for the legends. And they were indeed exciting!

From around the corner, she saw Vaughn and another man striding toward the hotel.

This must be Violet's brother, Joseph. A glance at the watch pinned to her dress told her it was just about time to meet them.

"It's time to go," she said to Nina, who was sharing her room.

They left the room, locking the door behind them

as Mama had always taught her, and Betsey placed the key in her reticule. Then they moved down the hall and down the stairs, in time to meet the men in the lobby.

"Cousin Betsey!" The dark-haired man beside Vaughn moved forward. With the same black hair as Violet and similar deep blue eyes, she would have known him anywhere.

"Cousin Joseph. I am so glad to see you in person." She was about to curtsy from habit, but he stepped forward and gave her a warm, brotherly hug.

She introduced her maid. "Nina has accompanied me on this trip."

"As she should. You had a safe journey?" he asked, after shaking Nina's hand. He gave Betsey his arm to escort her.

"Indeed. It was more pleasant than I anticipated," she answered, and they moved together to the restaurant room. Nina silently followed. "It gave me a chance to see many beautiful sights as we crossed the country." She'd traveled by rail, then this last part of the journey by stage, since the train didn't come as often as the stagecoaches.

Joseph pulled a chair out for her at a large table, then one for her maid. In New York City she would not have brought her maid along if she was visiting family; but Drew and Violet had insisted she not travel alone. Joe sat to her left, and Vaughn to her right next to Nina.

"We thought after traveling all day you might want to dine early," Joseph said, "and then, to retire early."

"That would be fine," she agreed. "We are both tired." She suspected she would sink into bed tonight and sleep immediately.

A young woman approached them. "Beef stew is

on the menu today," she told them. "And we have biscuits, and there's pie for dessert."

They ordered the stew, with Betsey and Nina requesting tea and the men asking for ale.

Betsey glanced around. Like the hotel, the eatery appeared clean, although plain compared to the lavish restaurants she had frequented in New York. She felt that someone was staring at her and turned to find Vaughn studying her.

She wondered what he saw. A woman who was pretty, she'd been told, but certainly not a raving beauty. She had dark blonde hair and hazel eyes and was short compared to many of her contemporaries. She liked dressing fashionably but had worn and packed her most serviceable clothing for this trip.

"We're very excited that you're here to help us with our search," Joseph began. He looked around, then lowered his voice. "Of course, we must be careful about what we say. The very walls sometimes have ears."

"Of course," Betsey replied, as the young woman returned with beer and her tea.

Vaughn grimaced as Joseph spoke. She challenged him. "Joseph said in his letter that you were not sure about this—quest."

"Oh, I'm sure about the quest," he replied, his voice gruff. "I'm just not sure about this method for—acquiring information." He gave his business partner a doubtful look, then focused on Betsey. "Or if you are the one to help us."

Chapter 2

Vaughn studied Miss Chalmers and her reaction to his words.

If she was startled or perturbed, she hid it well. Perhaps these society ladies were trained to mask their emotions.

She was beautiful, but not in a flamboyant way. Classical features, wide hazel eyes, and dark blonde hair that curled softly at her shoulders, would make any man sit up and take notice. And it appeared that under the fabric of her simple, yellow-flowered dress was a figure that had curves in all the right places.

While she appeared to be a citified woman, she seemed at home out here, as if she was fairly adaptable.

Too bad she—and Joseph—had some loco ideas.

Ten years ago, the Spaniard, Carlos Ayala, had been found dead, a knife in his back. That, after bragging all over the Cheyenne and Denver areas—and who knows where else—that he had found the richest mine of gold ever to be seen in the Medicine Bow Mountains. Perhaps the richest in the west. A gold mine rumored to be known of only by the Cheyenne Indians. He had returned to gather equipment and men to help him excavate.

Supposedly, the man they called The Spaniard had drawn a map and given it to a friend named Pedro, like hundreds of other men. But friend Pedro never came forward.

And the map was never found after Carlos' death.

Of course, many men had tried to find the mine. Some just ran off to look without a plan. Others calculated, did research on the area the Spaniard was rumored to have frequented, and then explored that area in a methodical manner.

He and Joseph had done so, exploring after their own research. To no avail.

No one had found any trace of the mine. Or the Spaniard's friend Pedro, either. Vaughn and Joseph had discovered Pedro's full name, Pedro Martinez, after speaking to dozens of people. But they'd never located the man. Had he met with foul play, as well?

Was it all a wild rumor?

Vaughn had been ready to give up. He wasn't lucky, and he and Joseph were doing all right in the carpentry and cabinet-making business they had started after pausing in their search. They had even hired on another man, Henry Gaston, and his son, Leon, to work for them in their shop.

And then Joseph had had his crazy idea.

Joseph's sister Violet had been involved in a number of séances with her now-husband, Drew, trying to contact Drew's murdered brother. They'd found out who the killer was, after numerous dead ends, and brought the killer to justice.

With Violet and Drew's abilities to conduct successful séances and speak to those who had passed on, Joseph proposed that they persuade them to come out west and conduct séances to contact the Spaniard and/or his friend, Pedro, if he had passed, too. So they could learn the location of the mine and bring the

Spaniard's killer to justice. Besides finding the gold, of course.

Vaughn had scoffed at the idea of contacting the departed.

Making contact with the dead, indeed! And even more preposterous—getting information from them!

While Vaughn's Indian mother, Singing Waters, had believed that the spirits of those who had passed still walked the earth on occasion, his father, Walter Montgomery, had been skeptical.

But Joseph had been like a man riding a runaway horse, holding on and refusing to let go of the idea. Joseph kept circling back to the notion, no matter how Vaughn tried to dissuade him. One day he announced he'd written to Violet and her husband, Drew, asking them to come here and conduct seances so they could speak to The Spaniard.

Weeks later, they got Violet's reply. She was expecting their first child and could not make the long trip.

Vaughn had felt relieved, figuring Joe would give up on his theory. Until Joe had continued to read Violet's letter aloud.

"But Drew's cousin, Betsey, has always wanted to visit the West," Violet wrote. "And since she recently lost her mother, she wants to travel even more so. It would be good for her. And," she had continued, "she was present at our most successful séances. We can offer her additional insights and training so she knows what to do. I approached her, and she is willing to come out and try."

Joseph had been ecstatic at the idea.

Vaughn, not so much.

He'd tried hard to persuade Joe to send another letter immediately, telling this cousin Betsey not to come out. But Joe had resisted, and before they knew it, she telegraphed that she was on her way.

And he must be insane to be going along with it.

Not that he'd had a lot of choice. Joe had sent for her before he even told Vaughn, and after Vaughn protested, Joseph still had refused to consider not attempting the seances.

So here they were.

He must have made some negative sound, because Betsey and Joe were staring at him now.

"Ugh…" He grabbed one of the warm biscuits the server had set before them and spread butter on it. "Don't you think it's unlikely that we'll be able to contact—either of the gentlemen we want to?" He directed his question first to Joe, then turned his head to look at Betsey.

"If I thought that, I wouldn't have asked her to come," Joe stated.

"If I thought that, I wouldn't have made the journey," Betsey said, "even though I really wanted to see this part of the country. And, so far, it's beautiful."

He nodded in agreement. "Wyoming is. But—this is a long shot." He glared at his business partner. What was Joseph thinking, to bring a city woman out here to conduct séances, of all things? Joe sounded more and more desperate.

"I'd like to rest tonight," Betsey said, as their server brought their stews. "Perhaps we can commence tomorrow evening?"

Joe nodded eagerly.

The food here was good, decent food and generous

portions. Vaughn silently dug into his stew, spearing a slice of potato.

"I can understand that. You've had a long journey," Joe said, sounding like he was still a bit impatient. "But then, I'd like to try our—experiment—tomorrow."

"And perhaps I can stroll around town tomorrow morning, seeing the sights," Betsey suggested, picking up a forkful of stew.

"We can take turns escorting you," Joe offered.

Vaughn nearly choked. Play nursemaid to a possibly spoiled city girl? Was his partner kidding? They had work to do.

"If we have the time," he warned his friend.

Betsey looked from one to another. "I'm sure I can stroll around town safely. Nina can come with me."

Nina, who had been silent during their conversation, nodded slowly.

"No—" Joe protested.

"No, you can't—" Vaughn interrupted. "Do you even have a gun? Or do you know how to use one?" He felt his body tense with anxiety. He didn't want her to come to harm, despite her unorthodox ideas.

Betsey's lips thinned. "As a matter of fact, my two older brothers taught me to use a gun, and we did range practice every summer when we were visiting upstate New York," she stated. She narrowed her eyes. "Surprised, Mr. Montgomery?"

"I'm glad to hear it," he said. Thank goodness for small favors.

"Very good," Joseph concurred. "Out here, ladies carry guns and know how to use them. The West is beautiful but can be a dangerous place, Betsey."

"So I hear." She took another forkful of meat. "I didn't bring one with me, though. I didn't think of bringing it."

Nina listened silently as they discussed guns.

"We'll buy you one," Vaughn stated. "And you too, Nina."

Betsey shot him a look he couldn't read.

Joe sat, nodding. He turned the conversation to his sisters, Violet and Rose, and Violet's new family. Betsey and Joseph spoke for several minutes about people he didn't know while Vaughn observed them both.

He gathered that Joseph, though he'd come out West to explore and in search of greener pastures, still missed his family and truly cared for his sisters.

"After the baby is born, maybe I'll go home to visit next year," Joseph said, surprising Vaughn. He sent him a glance. "As long as Vaughn can handle things while I'm gone. With the trip and all, it will probably be a few months."

"I can handle things," Vaughn declared. He hoped.

"Where are you from?" Betsey asked, sipping her tea and focusing her eyes on Vaughn. "I can tell by your speech you're not from the East."

"Nebraska." And he didn't want to elaborate on that.

"What made you decide to come out to Wylder?" she asked.

Escaping the town where he was a nobody. Worse than a nobody.

Aloud, he said, "I grew up on a small farm. My ma and pa died of the fever that was going around when I was seventeen, leaving me alone. I always wanted to see Wyoming—heard it was beautiful country, with lots of chances for a man to make his way—and decided to come out here." It was the story which often rolled off his tongue. Although it wasn't the whole story.

"Do you have any siblings?" Betsey asked.

He shook his head. "I had an older brother, who died shortly after my parents." He still felt a hollow place in his stomach when he thought of his older brother. They'd been over four years apart, but he'd looked up to him. He didn't want to go into the story of Victor's death.

"I am sorry." Betsey stared at him. "I lost my mother recently and my father years ago; but it must be difficult to have no one left in the family."

Vaughn shrugged. "Joseph's become—almost a brother," he said.

Joe grinned.

Betsey smiled, too. "I'm glad. Everyone needs some friends and family."

Not me, he thought.

But Joe was beaming at him. "I only have sisters, and Vaughn is the closest thing to a brother I've ever had."

Slightly embarrassed, Vaughn looked away.

"Your sister, Violet, has become a sister to me," Betsey told Joe with a wide smile. "I love her."

Joe's smile grew even wider.

"I have only my older brothers," Betsey added.

Enough with these family compliments. Vaughn shifted in his chair and drank some more ale. "Do you really think you can successfully contact the dead?" he challenged but kept his voice low.

"You seem to be quite the skeptic, Mr.

Montgomery," Betsey said, reverting to his last name, her eyebrows raised at him.

"I am."

"Well, I can tell you we had a lot of successes in the past. We were able to contact—after numerous tries—my cousin Drew's brother, and our success helped us reveal the identity of his killer. And other entities came through, too," Betsey assured them. "For example, Joseph, an old neighbor of yours—Eddie O'Rourke—visited us on occasion."

"You don't say? I always liked Eddie and was sad to learn he'd passed." Joe sipped his ale.

She smiled. "He was quite a congenial man. And Drew's mother, Claire, and one of Drew's employees showed up on different occasions. Of course, we had the help of an experienced medium sometimes, and Drew himself is quite learned in topics of the occult. But he felt confident that I could conduct séances and be able to help you," she said, her voice rising in a challenge.

Vaughn harrumphed. "We shall see."

Chapter 3

The following morning, Betsey awoke early, having had a good and restful night.

She and Nina had gone to bed early, tired from their travels. The room included two beds, which was somewhat of a luxury. In some of the places she'd stayed while traveling, Betsey had had to share one bed with Nina, which meant she did not get as good a night's sleep. Her maid was a restless sleeper, and often bumped into Betsey during the night. At least here the noise from the street—horses, people calling to each other, some laughter—didn't bother her. She was used to the hustle and bustle of New York City at night, and this town was much quieter by comparison. Also, at some point during the night, it became very quiet. She guessed that people in Wyoming went to bed earlier than in New York City. So between less noise and her own bed, she'd fallen into a deep, undisturbed sleep.

During her travels, she had slept on trains, snoozed on stagecoaches, and slept in various posting inns. Now that she was here—at least for a few weeks in the same spot—the hotel would be her home base. Her room had a sitting room, as she'd requested, with chairs and a table she could use for their séances. She'd tumbled into bed feeling weary but satisfied last night since she had arrived at her destination, and all appeared in order.

Now, Betsey washed and dressed and went in

search of breakfast with Nina.

Joseph had told her he and Vaughn rose early and usually got to work immediately, with full days ahead, although they sometimes could sneak in short naps in the afternoon. The plan for Betsey's first day was for Vaughn to ride out in the morning with Betsey and show her some of the countryside. Nina didn't care for riding much so she would stay in the hotel. Then, in the afternoon, Joseph would escort Betsey and Nina around town so they could see shops, get the lay of the land, and perhaps—a peek at a saloon or two, which Betsey was curious about.

She had, of course, caught glimpses of saloons at the places they'd stopped as they traveled—like Dodge City in Kansas and Denver in Colorado. There was great beauty out here in the West, but people seemed to drink just as much as they did in New York.

She couldn't wait to explore Wyoming.

Not to mention she was so intrigued by the idea of a lost treasure!

She didn't mind eating breakfast with only Nina. She'd grown used to eating by herself since her mother had passed, and, of course, at home Nina ate her meals with the other servants. Betsey's two older brothers lived in their own homes with their families.

Entering the restaurant, Betsey found a handful of people already there. A middle-aged man with a younger woman who resembled him—probably his daughter. Two businessmen. A couple in their thirties, she thought, who spoke in low tones with decidedly British accents.

She and Nina were finishing breakfast—which was quite good—when she saw Vaughn walk into the room.

Heads turned.

People noticed him, she observed. Whether it was his handsome face, the masculine set of his shoulders, or something less definable—an air about him, a look of somehow being in charge—both women and men noticed this man. Betsey felt herself tense up as she observed him.

She was just as conscious of the man as any woman here.

Hastily, she finished her coffee.

"I'm almost ready," she said to him.

He nodded. "I'm a mite early. I'll have some coffee," he told the girl working at the restaurant.

While he drank his coffee, Betsey went up to her room to finish getting ready and was back downstairs in less than ten minutes, at the time they'd originally agreed to meet. Nina stayed upstairs. "I'll feel safer if I stay in our rooms," she said to Betsey. She didn't like reading as much as Betsey did, but she'd brought along her knitting, and already she had completed several winter scarves during their journey.

Betsey went downstairs, her stomach fluttering as if butterflies were taking flight inside. She took Vaughn's offered arm, and he escorted her to the stables. She liked the feel of her hand in the crook of his arm as they walked.

She was impressed by the stables here in Wylder. They were larger than many she'd seen and were clean and in good condition.

"You have much experience riding?" Vaughn asked.

She met his gaze. "Enough. We don't ride much in the city, but I always rode when we went upstate in the summer; I've ridden out with my cousins in New Jersey during the summer, too. Drew has a couple of horses stabled in town."

"That's good." He nodded.

He helped her up onto the brown horse, named Lady, and swung onto his black stallion, whom he said was named Chief.

They walked their horses through the town. Betsey observed the usual general goods store, a saloon, a milliner, the telegraph office, a bank, church, a blacksmith, and the doctor. There appeared to be more businesses around the corner, too.

Several people waved at Vaughn and tipped their hats to her. As they passed, he pointed out the Reverend Thomas who waved from the steps of the church and Mrs. Bimby, a local, older woman who lived near his shop.

They settled into a nice, easy trot over a trail that passed by a wooded area.

"We're going out to Blue Lake," he told her, as they rode north. "It's a nice lake not far from here, where people go swimming and picnicking during the summer. Even in fall, it's a popular spot."

She watched him as he talked. His face, which had been serious, seemed more relaxed as he rode. She asked him about the mountains that were in the background, and he told her they were the Medicine Bow Mountains, where the treasure was rumored to be.

"There's a lot of stories and legends associated with those mountains," he said. "Not the least of which is the legend of the Spaniard's Mine."

"And where there's smoke, there's usually fire," Betsey said. She stared at the mountains in the distance, already green with sprouting bushes and trees, and a shiver swept up her spine. She could just imagine the stories of hauntings and such.

"Are there any ghost stories about them?" she asked.

"Enough." He shrugged. "When I first came out here, even before I met Joe, I heard tales of ghosts who had been heard wailing at night and spirits seen by men who were credible. Most of the mountains in the West seem to have their own ghost stories. Like the Superstition Mountains in Arizona. But," he added, "it's probably just a lot of hooey."

"Don't be so sure. I've seen things at séances that would surprise you," Betsey said solemnly.

"I don't believe you can bring back the dead."

"Perhaps you'll change your mind," she challenged. Inside her brain was screaming, don't be so skeptical.

He grimaced. "Doubt it."

They fell silent, and about fifteen minutes later, they reached the lake. The water was a lovely blue and sparkled in the sunshine. Trees grew around the lake, which was a good size, and she spotted the creek which fed into it.

"That's Blue Creek," Vaughn said as he dismounted.

"It's very picturesque." There were flowers growing nearby, too, and Betsey had a sudden urge to paint the scene. Surprised, she welcomed the urge. She hadn't wanted to paint since her dear mother had passed. "I feel like—painting again."

"Again?" He raised his eyebrows.

"I used to enjoy it…but I haven't painted since my

mother passed last year. I just—lost the desire to." A wave of sadness flowed through her as she remembered her mother, who'd become more and more frail, finally succumbing to a bout of pneumonia.

"You miss her." There was sympathy in his voice.

"Yes. My brothers are both married and busy with their families. And I don't see my cousins as much as I would like. As I mentioned, I have no sisters, although Violet has become like a sister to me."

He nodded and helped her down from Lady.

They led their horses to the lake, where the animals both drank. Betsey stared at the clear, blue water. "Violet and Drew's baby is due in about a month. I can't wait to hear the good news when he or she arrives."

She turned to look at Vaughn. "This is a very beautiful area. What made you settle in Wylder with all of Wyoming to choose from?'

He gazed at the lake, but Betsey thought he was seeing scenes from another place, another time. "Once I came out here, the magnificence of Wyoming got to me. It was beautiful, colorful—everything I'd heard about. This area might get a lot of snow, but all the seasons are beautiful, and the summers are very comfortable. After traveling around Wyoming, this town called to me, and I decided to settle here."

The horses finished drinking, and he loped their reins loosely over a tree branch, leaving them to graze on the grass.

"How did you meet Joseph?"

He grinned. "I had traveled to Phoenix to look at some horses there and was in a saloon for a drink, when Joe walked in. I was drinking with a man named

Nathaniel, and Joe knew him because they'd prospected in Nevada together. Nathaniel introduced him. I liked Joe at once, and we just hit it off. After a few days of drinking and poker, Joe persuaded me to try some prospecting with him. Nathaniel was headed up to Colorado, so Joe and I went out alone. Then we tried our luck in Wyoming. We didn't find anything, but during those few months we got to know each other real well. I told him how much I liked Wylder, and he agreed to come here."

He turned to her. "We learned we both had some carpentry experience and enjoyed it. We also were good enough to make custom wood furniture. We decided to start a business here. Wylder didn't have a carpentry business, despite having a lumber company; people had to go over to another town to get custom cabinets. We turned an old building into our shop, and we got the business going a couple of years ago."

"And do you like it?" she asked as they walked along the banks of the lake. She brushed away an insect buzzing by her ear. She was enjoying this quiet time with Vaughn.

"Very much. We take orders, but most of the work is on our own. We don't have to speak to a lot of people daily."

Well, that sounded dark. It was her turn to raise her eyebrows at him. "Really?"

"Really." He grinned suddenly. "I suppose you're going to tell me people are wonderful."

"Actually, I've met some who weren't," she said frankly, meeting his eyes. "Such as the woman who tried to kill my cousins. She was pure evil."

"A woman, huh? I've met men like that, but not

too many women," he acknowledged.

"There are bad apples of both sexes."

"True enough." He bent down, picked up a flat rock, and threw it, watching it skim over the surface of the lake before sinking with a splash. Then he turned to her.

When his deep brown eyes met hers, awareness shimmied up her spine. An awareness of being alone with a handsome man.

An intriguing man, too. There was something mysterious about Vaughn Montgomery.

She swallowed. It had been a long time since she was alone with a man who was so handsome and masculine. She couldn't even remember the last time.

Was that why her heart was suddenly beating faster?

Chapter 4

Suddenly self-conscious, Betsey turned away, her cheeks growing warm. "So you think you'll stay out here?" She felt her cheeks warm with embarrassment. She sounded like a young miss speaking to a potential sweetheart for the first time.

"Yes. There's nothing left for me in Nebraska." The words sounded rather harsh.

She turned back to him, studying him. There wasn't merely the sadness of loss in his voice. There was something else. Something—bitter.

Again, he met her eyes. But he said nothing more.

"Well, you have a good friend in Joe, if he's anything like his sisters. I've met Rose, too, and she and Violet are exceedingly good-natured, kind, and loyal," she stated.

"Joe is all of those things," he agreed quietly. He turned to regard the lake again. "Not many men are as good-hearted as him. And out here in the West, among all the good men, there are some bad, twisted men, too. You should beware of them, Miz Chalmers."

She took a step closer. "Please, call me Betsey."

"Betsey. There's a lot of lawlessness out here. Men who want to take advantage of others, who want to grab what isn't theirs. With less of the law out this way, it can be a dangerous place."

"I'm not afraid," she told him. "New York City can

be a dangerous sort of place, too."

He glanced at her, frowning. "But you probably had friends and family to protect you. And servants, like Nina."

She shrugged. "It is perfectly safe to go about during the day, even alone. As long as you know your way around the great city. At night, of course, I only went out with friends, or family, or an escort."

"It's a lot less safe out here," he insisted.

She wondered if he was trying to warn her. From…what? The wild, wicked West? Or something else?

He drew closer. "Don't go anywhere alone," he said firmly. "Make sure Joe or I or Nina are with you."

"I won't." It would be foolish, she knew, to wander about a part of the country she barely knew.

She tilted her head up to look him squarely in the eyes as she answered him. Once again something flared inside of her. Like a warm fire in winter. She was intensely aware of this man, the sound of his husky voice, his good looks, and the clean smell of his skin when she was near. He wore rather worn clothes that bespoke a hard-working person. She surmised he was ambitious as well as industrious. .

Despite the older-looking clothes, he still looked handsome. It all added up to an appealing total.

He reached down and plucked one of the flowers from the bunch growing near a tree. Betsey did not recognize the yellow blooms.

"Here, pretty lady," he said it solemnly.

Something warm rushed through her. "Thank you, kind sir," she quipped and took the flower from his hand. She bent her head and sniffed the subtle fragrance.

"What is it?" she asked.

"I dunno. But they grow hereabouts." Again, he met her eyes, and warmth flowed through her. She felt as sparkling as the water in the Blue Lake.

"It's lovely." She smiled up at him, conscious of how he towered over her. She knew she was five foot four inches, and he had to be at least six feet, maybe a little taller.

He smiled briefly, then turned back to the lake. "This lake reminds me of a lake near my grandparents' farm."

"Tell me about it," she said softly, curious about this man's past.

"Not much to tell. Grandma and Grandpa Montgomery were my father's folks. They had a small but prosperous farm. My father was one of five children, so often when we visited—they were about two hours by wagon from our home—there would be other cousins visiting there, too. My brother and I loved to go and play there." His voice sounded warm, as if the memories were sweet. "Eventually one of my cousins, Leroy, came out west, too, and I ran into him in New Mexico a few years back."

"How nice. Have you kept in touch?" she asked.

His face shuttered. "No. He headed up to Montana last I heard." He turned. "C'mon, let's ride out a little further. I'll show you the Holt ranch, the biggest spread in the area."

They strolled back to the horses. Vaughn helped her up, and she noticed how careful he was when he did so, and how well he treated the horses, gently but firm.

They rode silently for the next several minutes.

Then they came to a ranch, with a long and low white house, a bunkhouse, and several barns. They rode past the well-maintained buildings and headed back to town on a different trail.

"Now, at least, you'll know how to get to the lake and the largest ranch hereabouts," he said as they rode back. "In a few days, Joe will ride out with you again."

As they rode into town, they passed a couple who waved, who Vaughn said were Mr. And Mrs. Greely.

A woman started waving madly as they approached the livery stable. She had pale blonde hair and was dressed in an elegant blue dress with red flowers, a straw hat with blue ribbons perched on her head. "Mr. Montgomery!" she called, her voice shrill.

A shadow passed over his face. Then Vaughn nodded and tipped his hat as they approached the woman. "Miz Lewis." He turned slightly to Betsey. "This is Miz Betsey Chalmers, Joseph's cousin." His voice was stiff as he indicated Betsey. So, she noted, was his posture, all of a sudden. He did not like Miss Lewis, she surmised. "Betsey, Miz Lewis." He paused the horse as the woman practically stepped in its path.

"Ramona Lewis. Pleased to meet you," the woman said, her tone cool. But she didn't sound pleased at all. She had narrowed her eyes and was staring up at Betsey.

Betsey suddenly felt plain in her basic cocoa-colored dress. She'd brought along mostly her older, serviceable clothes, hearing that the West was not only more casual, but that clothes got dusty quickly out here. There was no sense in ruining her smart New York gowns and fancier dresses.

"Nice to meet you," Betsey replied, trying to put

some friendliness into her voice.

The woman turned to Vaughn, and this time her voice was warm as sunshine. "I was going to drop by the cabinet shop to talk to you about making another dressing table for me. This time I think I want a larger one. I can put the other one in our guestroom, since it is still in excellent shape."

"That's fine, Miz Lewis," he answered.

"Perhaps we can go for a ride later," she added.

"Sorry, I have work to do for the rest of the day," Vaughn answered.

She frowned. Then, relaxing her mouth, she continued, "Perhaps another time?"

"Perhaps." He sounded decidedly noncommittal, Betsey thought. He started to ride again, and Betsey kept up with him.

"Good day," the woman said, gazing at Vaughn.

"Good day," Betsey echoed to the young woman.

When they'd gone farther down the street, she asked Vaughn, "Do you not like Miss Lewis?"

"Not particularly," he admitted. "I once saw her try to kick a dog which was barking, and she pushed a child aside another time, and the poor girl went tumbling into the street and hurt her leg."

"How awful," Betsey exclaimed. "I can't abide those who are hurtful to animals or children."

"I feel likewise," he said.

They came to the livery stable. A man stepped out and helped Betsey down as Vaughn swung off his horse.

"Thank you for showing me around," Betsey said to Vaughn, smiling.

"You're welcome." His voice was a little gruff as

he turned to her. "I'll escort you to the hotel. Joe and I usually have a quick lunch in our back room. Why don't you and your maid join us for lunch in fifteen minutes? Afterwards, Joe wants to show you around the town."

"That will be fine," she agreed.

They saw no sign of Miss Lewis as Vaughn escorted her back to the hotel.

Once she'd freshened up and had Nina with her, she easily found her way to the cabinet shop. After a brief lunch of sandwiches with her cousin and Vaughn, where they discussed the highlights of what she's seen this morning, Betsey opened her parasol against the bright Wyoming sunshine. With the sun high in the sky, there was a strong glare. Besides, she didn't want her skin to be burned, as her Aunt Patricia had warned her could happen.

They strolled in a leisurely fashion, Nina wanting a tour also. Joe introduced her to Cassandra, who owned the millinery store. The store featured some lovely hats, and Betsey determined to buy one while she was in Wylder. She wanted to support the woman's business. They went into the general mercantile, and she met the owners, who were members of the Wylder family. The store was larger than she'd thought at first. The owners were friendly, and the store featured quite a variety of household goods, foods, supplies, and even fabrics for dresses.

As they exited the store, a young woman of about Betsey's age, or perhaps a little younger, was approaching.

"Joe," she called eagerly.

He turned, smiling widely at the young lady.

"Millie!" He moved towards her. Then, as if remembering Betsey, he turned back. "Millie, may I present my cousin Betsey Chalmers? This is Miss Millicent Haynes, a—friend."

Betsey noticed the slight hesitation over the woman's status. The woman, a petite brunette with freckles, smiled widely at her. She was dressed in a light-green frock, which Betsey recognized as a popular style from the preceding year. So, even out here, they tried to follow fashion trends. The woman appeared much friendlier than the cool woman, Ramona Lewis, whom she'd met this morning. "And this is my maid, Nina." She tried hard to include Nina and not make her feel like an afterthought.

"I am so pleased to meet Joe's cousin!" Millie exclaimed. "And you, too, Nina. Oh, I know you're not exactly cousins, Betsey; his sister married your cousin. But that's close enough, especially out here, where we've all become family." She beamed.

Betsey found herself smiling back. "I'm happy to meet you, too," she said.

Millie turned to regard Joe, and the adoring look in her eyes caught Betsey by surprise. It was obvious that this young woman had feelings for him. Betsey turned slightly to look at him and saw his expression was similar. Joe was looking at Millie as if he cared for her. A lot.

"Millicent Mae!" a sharp voice called from down the street.

All four of them turned to see a stout woman in a dark-purple dress bearing down on them. The woman was older and frowning. Millie's mother, perhaps?

Millie flushed and looked disappointed at the

interruption.

Joe tipped his hat. "Mrs. Haynes, may I present my cousin from New York City, Miss Betsey Chalmers?"

"New York City?" The woman sounded as if she was impressed but reluctant to be so. She drew closer. "How do you do, Miss Chalmers." Her voice had become gracious.

"A pleasure to meet you," Betsey said, giving the woman a wide smile. "And this is my maid, Nina Smith."

Mrs. Haynes stared for a moment at Nina, then looked at Betsey with an approving smile. Apparently, having a lady's maid out here made Betsey go up in the woman's estimation; Betsey could see her calculating in her mind that Betsey must be of the upper class, well able to afford such luxuries.

After giving Betsey a gracious smile and nod, Mrs. Haynes turned to regard her daughter. "Come along, Millicent," she snapped and started to lead the way back up the street.

Millie sent Joe an entreating look, then hurried after her mother, who was marching briskly. "Mother!" she called, sounding annoyed.

Mrs. Haynes kept going. Once Millie caught up to her, there were some angrily whispered words which Betsey couldn't distinguish. The *clip-clop* of horses pulling a passing wagon drowned out their voices.

She turned back to Joe. He was gazing after Millie, a bemused expression on his face.

Betsey touched his arm lightly. "You care for her, don't you?" She kept her voice low.

He flushed. "I—yes." He took Betsey's arm, and they continued down the street, but at a more leisurely pace than the Haynes. "But Mr. And Mrs. Haynes don't approve of me. They feel a cabinet maker, while he might make a decent living, does not have enough money to be wealthy. They've set their sights on a widower, Harold Totten, for Millie. His family is very—prestigious." Joe's voice faltered.

"And she cares about you, too," Betsey said sympathetically. "I can see it. So—why listen to her family? Why don't you just get married anyway?"

He set his mouth in a line. "After we find the gold, I'll have plenty to offer her, and her parents will see me in a different light. Now let's go buy you two women guns."

Betsey stared at him as he pointed them toward the gunsmith's shop.

She *hoped* they were able to find the gold!

Chapter 5

Betsey lit the candles on the round table. A small breeze stirred the curtains in the sitting room which was part of her suite, as the sun finished setting in a spectacular show of roses and purples and orange. She had seen some paints and brushes at the general store, and she determined to buy them tomorrow. She itched to capture some of the beauty of the West on canvas.

Now, though, she had a different task ahead of her. She glanced around the room. In the softening twilight, the chairs and table with the dark-blue cloth were waiting, inviting them to sit. She'd lowered the oil lamp on the side table so there would be very little light in the room. Her cousin Drew liked to leave the windows open, even if it was just a little, because he felt it helped the spirits feel welcome. Betsey had placed paper and a pen nearby, to make notes immediately after the séance. During Drew's experiments, they found it was better to take notes right after the séance than during the actual proceedings. Now she surveyed the room, feeling satisfied and eager to see whom they might contact.

There was a knock on the door. The clock on the mantle said it was almost eight. The men were on time.

Betsey smoothed her hands over her hair one last time, then opened the door.

"Hi, cousin," Joe said in his jovial voice.

"Hello." Vaughn's voice was subdued, and his

mouth set in a straight, skeptical line.

"Please, have a seat." She waved toward the table, feeling that familiar fluttering inside she always felt when she was near Vaughn.

Joe noted the open window. "Violet said you like to leave windows open, even if it's only little bit."

"Yes. Drew believes it shows the spirits they are welcome," Betsey said and took a seat.

Vaughn gave a snort.

When she looked at him, he looked embarrassed. "Sorry," he mumbled. "I still don't believe in any of this stuff." He looked down.

Nina entered from the bedroom, and quietly took a seat.

It had turned dark outside. The candle flames danced in the slight breeze. She could hear the *clip-clop* of several horses from the street, and someone called "Hey, Billy!" She went to close the window farther, leaving only a small section open.

"Now," she began, "let us hold hands. Drew believes that helps."

She took hold of Nina's in her right hand and Vaughn's in her left. Vaughn's large hands were rough. Years of hard work, she recognized.

Nina had not attended any of their previous seances. Now, she frowned, her face creased with worry.

"Let us think of the Spaniard," Betsey whispered. "Spirits, we appeal to you, we seek the Spaniard, Carlos Ayala, for information."

All was quiet. In the pale light from the candles and the low oil lamp, nothing moved. The very air seemed still.

They waited. After about five minutes, Betsey sensed the heaviness in the air that she and Violet had often noticed when an entity was nearby. As if some air was displaced by a person or being.

"Top of the evenin' to you, folks!" came the familiar and genial tones from out of the dark.

Chapter 6

"Eddie?" Joe gasped.

"Eddie O'Rourke?" Betsey exclaimed at the same time. Delight flowed through her. He was a familiar entity.

Nina sat up straighter, her mouth open.

"Glad to see you again, young lady," the man's spirit declared in his jovial voice.

Betsey could smell the cigar that usually accompanied his spirit. He was a neighbor of Joe's family, a man they had liked very much when he was alive. Joe's sister, Violet, had contacted him by accident in the past, when they were searching for the killer of Drew's brother, Charles. Betsey was surprised that apparently, Eddie was still hanging around the Moore siblings and their friends.

She cast a glance at Vaughn. He was sitting stiffly, and he looked, not quite stunned, but definitely surprised. Then, as he met her glance, the look was carefully wiped away, as if he didn't want her to know he was taken aback. Still holding hands, he bent to look under the table.

Eddie laughed. "I see your friend over here is a skeptic," he said, his voice coming from close to Joe.

Vaughn sat upright, and even in the dark Betsey thought he looked flushed. "I am skeptical," he snapped. "There are a lot of charlatans out there."

"Oh, ho, friend! There are some. This young lady is not one of them." A wisp of smoke drifted near Joe's ear. "Well, Joey me boy, let me tell you I've been around your sisters. With them both increasing, I wanted to pop in on 'em and check to see how they're doing. Both Violet and Rose look lovely and feel well."

"Thanks for looking out for them," Joe said.

"Yes, thanks," Betsey echoed. She hesitated, then asked softly, "We're trying to reach someone called The Spaniard. We want to ask him, or his friend Pedro, questions about a gold mine they discovered."

There was a long pause, and Betsey feared Eddie had disappeared. Then, he said, "No one else here tonight who can come through. I'll nose around, though, and see if I can find the blokes."

Vaughn raised his eyebrows.

Nina sat silently, her mouth remaining open.

Betsey nodded, hoping Vaughn wouldn't say something disparaging. "Very good, Eddie. It's always good to—to hear from you."

"Night, folks." And the air lightened, as a wisp of smoke drifted by her face.

"Goodnight," Betsey murmured, as Joe said, "Goodnight, Eddie!"

Both Vaughn and Nina sat there, staring at the space where the voice had come from.

"Well, that was exciting!" Joe said after a minute of silence passed. "Violet wrote to me and said he came through several times for you all in New Jersey."

"Yes, he did," Betsey affirmed. "He was always so nice. He cares for your family, and he seems to have contact with other spirits. He seems to be watching over you all."

"Really?" Vaughn's skeptical voice echoed in the room.

She sighed. "I believe we will have no more visits tonight. The air is no longer heavy. Although we can wait a few minutes."

"Yes, let's wait," Joe urged.

They sat in silence for five minutes. Betsey noticed Vaughn's face was set, as if he was a marble statue.

Then Joe shifted in his seat. "Guess that's it for tonight," he stated. "But—that was amazing! We actually had contact with someone who's departed!"

Betsey nodded. "Yes."

Vaughn stared at Joe, then turned to look at her.

"This is hard to believe," he said. His expression bespoke disbelief and wariness.

"You think she's staged this?" Joe asked. He sounded angry.

"Well—" Vaughn had the grace to look embarrassed. "No, I don't think Betsey's doing any theatrical stuff. But maybe, Joe, you were hypnotized or something—"

"I watched her prepare," Nina spoke up. "Miss Betsey only laid out candles and such. There was no trickery involved."

"Of course I wouldn't do anything like that!" Betsey declared, indignant. How dare Vaughn suggest such a thing? And she was grateful for her maid's loyalty.

"Hogwash," Joe protested. "Betsey would never do anything of the sort. Besides, they had huge successes back in New Jersey. They even caught Charlie's killer. She has no reason to stage anything."

Vaughn shrugged, still looking dubious. "I meant

no personal criticism of Betsey."

"Did you not?" She couldn't keep the tinge of sarcasm from her voice.

Vaughn met her eyes, and they stared at each other. He dropped his first.

"We will try again tomorrow," she said smoothly, trying to draw on an appearance of total confidence. Meanwhile, she felt a wave of relief. At least she had had some small success tonight on her own, without Violet and Drew being present. She had proven to herself she could conduct a séance!

"You want to attempt a séance again so soon?" Vaughn asked.

She turned to face him head on. "Yes. You *do* want to find the Spaniard's Mine, don't you?"

"Yes. I'm just not sure this is the way to do it," he stated.

Nina stared at him. Betsey suspected her lady's maid was wondering why, if he was so uncertain, Betsey and she had made the journey west.

"Well, we will certainly try," Betsey said dryly. She moved to the oil lamp and turned the light up. "Tomorrow, at the same time, if that is acceptable to you both."

Joe stood and gave her a big hug. As they were leaving, Vaughn glanced over his shoulder with an enigmatic look.

She closed the door after them and sighed. "You may go to bed," she told Nina. "I shall write down notes on what happened tonight." She got busy making those notes promptly, while Nina prepared to turn in. Betsey's cousin Drew had taught her to make careful notes so they could scientifically document the occurrence at these séances. Finally, Betsey wrote a letter to Violet and Drew, detailing what had happened since her arrival in Wylder and about the first séance she had conducted with Joe and Vaughn and Nina in attendance.

She prepared to go to sleep afterwards, spending a few minutes in a comfortable chair reading one of the books Drew had given her on séances. She felt tired and soon turned in for the night.

She didn't fall asleep immediately. Nina snored slightly in the next bed. Betsey lay there, pondering Vaughn Montgomery. Why, she wondered, was he so skeptical about her and the séances? Perhaps he didn't trust women? Or had a closed mind?

It was a while before she fell asleep. She did sleep deeply and awoke at her usual time, seven thirty, to find a gray day outside her window.

After breakfast with Nina, they walked over to the small post office and sent the letter to Violet and Drew. Then she went back to her room to read more of the séance book. But she felt restless, so she finally said to Nina, "I want to take a walk."

"I will go with you, Miss Betsey," the woman said in a quiet tone. She'd always stuck to Betsey since they left New York. Betsey didn't know if she did it out of loyalty, because she'd promised Betsey's brothers to stick close by, or because she was worried about the "dangers of the West to a woman alone" as one of her sisters-in-law had phrased it.

The wind whipped her hair, and the air felt damp as they left the hotel. She knew the promise of rain was a much-needed event out here. She'd even heard from a fellow traveler that some Indian tribes did dances, hoping to please their Gods and bring on rain. Joseph had also mentioned they hadn't had rain for several weeks. So a gray day was welcomed by the residents.

A few people greeted her as she passed. She considered going over to the woodworking and cabinet shop, but she realized that Joe and Vaughn were probably busy at this hour. She could see a man and woman going in there, and another man left carrying a small wooden chair that looked, even from a distance, like it was intricately carved.

She turned away and almost bumped into a well-dressed man coming down the street.

"Pardon me, ma'am," he said, tipping his hat.

He looked rather like some of the gamblers she'd seen at a few saloons, dressed in nice, clean, fashionable clothes like the newer styles from the East. He had light-brown hair and a moustache and grayish blue eyes.

"It was my fault," Betsey said.

"No, indeed, the fault was all mine." He smiled a charming smile. "You're new hereabouts, aren't you? My name is Sims, Haskell Sims, and I live with my sister just around the corner from here."

"Betsey Chalmers, and this is Nina." She extended her hand, as she had seen done in the West, and they shook. Nina bobbed a curtsey. "I don't believe I have met your sister yet."

"I just returned from a trip to New Orleans," he said smoothly. "So I have not been out and about with her for weeks."

She wondered if that included gambling, since the city was known for its roulette wheels and poker games.

"My sister Louisa lives here year-round."

Betsey nodded. "Perhaps I will meet her soon."

"And what brings you to our lovely town?" he said, falling into step with her as she moved down the boardwalk. Nina followed them.

"I am visiting my cousin, Joseph Moore," Betsey said. It was what they had decided to tell people before she even came out here. Some people were superstitious and believed séances were a bad thing; on top of that, Joey and Vaughn did not want people to know they were still searching for the Spaniard's Mine. The less said, they'd all agreed, the better. "I've always had a desire to see the West; and since my mother died recently, it seemed an opportune time to visit," she finished.

"You have my condolences," Mr. Sims remarked. He held out his arm. "Care to join me in my walk?"

"Thank you." She accepted his arm, catching the scent of a sandalwood soap he must be using. As they strolled down the street, Millie was coming down the street from the opposite direction. Nina silently followed.

"Miss Haynes," he drawled to Millie in his pleasant voice.

"I was going to the milliner's," Millie called to Betsey. "Do you want to join me?" She drew abreast of them.

"That's where I was headed!" Betsey said, smiling. She turned to Mr. Sims. "Nice to meet you, Mr. Sims."

"Haskell," he corrected. "I hope to see all you ladies at the social on Saturday." He gave a brief bow, then continued down the street.

Millie took Betsey's elbow and led her to the milliner's shop. "I understand she just got a new shipment of ribbons, and I am hoping to buy a new hat."

"I wanted to get one while I'm here, too," Betsey said. "What social is he talking about?"

"Haven't Joey and Vaughn told you?" Millie raised her eyebrows. "Men!" She laughed. "There's to be a social at the Brown's barn this Saturday. To celebrate the birth of their grandson several weeks ago. The whole town is invited." She sighed. "Those men! You'd think Joe and Vaughn would have remembered to tell you. I even reminded Joe a few days ago."

How typical, Betsey mused, for them to forget to tell her and Nina about a social gathering. She recalled her sisters-in-law often complained about their husbands, Betsey's brothers, doing the same.

"That sounds like fun," Betsey said. "Do we get dressed up?"

"Of course!" Millie said. "And you come, too," she said, directing her remarks to Nina. "Everyone's invited."

Chatting, they went to look at the hats on display at the milliners. Mrs. Carter came out and showed them a few new designs she was working on and the new ribbons which had arrived. Betsey selected a design she liked and ordered it to be made with the turquoise ribbon that the milliner had just obtained. Millie ordered a hat with emerald green ribbons.

"I shall have them ready for you in a week, perhaps less," the milliner promised, looking pleased with their orders.

"That will be fine," Betsey said.

They left the shop. Millie slipped her arm into Betsey's. "Why don't we have lunch at the restaurant down the street? Sally and her mother run it," she spoke loudly as a large stagecoach rumbled by.

Once the three women were seated at the table and had ordered the chicken soup and fresh bread that were being served for lunch, Millie leaned in close to Betsey. "Did you have any success last night?"

"Success?" Betsey asked, surprised.

Millie lowered her voice even more. "Joe told me you are…pursuing a rather…unorthodox way to get information." Her eyes gleamed with excitement.

So…Joey had said something to Millie. Betsey stared at Millie. Wasn't this supposed to be hush-hush?

"Of course, he told me in confidence," Millie said hastily. "I would not breathe a word to anyone. Although, everyone does know that he and Vaughn have been looking for the Spaniard's Mine for over a year."

Betsey sat back. "I am sworn to secrecy."

"But I already know," Millie persisted. Then she sighed. "I suppose you have to be close-mouthed about it. We will say no more."

"I can tell you—we did not have complete success," Betsey said slowly.

"Oh dear." Millie frowned

"But—something good happened."

"Really?"

"I'll have to speak with Joe and Vaughn before I can say any more," Betsey told her primly. She liked Millie and didn't want to keep secrets from her—but she was obligated first to Joe and Vaughn.

"I understand," Millie said, as a young woman brought over their soups and aromatic bread.

"You know, the West has become a much more

civilized place now that it's the 1890s," Millie said, dipping her spoon in the broth loaded with bits of chicken and vegetables. It smelled delicious, and Betsey took hold of her own spoon.

"So I've been told. I do hope people are—more open-minded about the occult, as they are back East. Why, in Canada—" she paused, as Haskell Sims entered the eatery.

"Hello, ladies," he said, removing his hat. He then moved over to another table where an older gentleman, also dressed in fashionable clothes, was waiting.

Mr. Simms dropped into a seat beside the gentleman and bent forward, their words hushed.

Betsey turned back to Millie. Millie grinned. "Haskell Sims is a very good-looking man, isn't he?" She must have seen Betsey's startled expression, because she continued hastily, "not that I'm interested in him. My heart belongs to Joe." Her voice dropped. And her expression looked wistful.

"I thought so." Betsey felt satisfaction wash over her. Millie seemed like a nice person, just like Joe. They would make a good match, she thought.

Millie flushed. "But my mother—" She leaned forward. "She wants me to marry someone wealthy. Like a banker or an older landowner. Like Mr. Madison, a widowed landowner in the next town." She frowned. "He's almost old enough to be my father. I don't want to marry someone like that."

"I don't blame you." Betsey sipped more of the delicious broth from her spoon. "I, too, hope to marry someday, for love." An image of Vaughn Montgomery flashed across her mind.

Now why was she thinking of him in that way?

"Joe is sweet on me, too," Millie whispered. "He—confided in me about how you are helping with his *search*. I'm sure he doesn't discuss that with anyone else except for you and Vaughn."

"Yes. Now, tell me, what do you think of the hat I ordered?" Betsey tried to turn the conversation to fashion.

Millie went along with the change in topics, and they chatted about fashions while finishing their lunch. Even the quiet Nina made some comments. After paying—Millie insisted on paying for them all—they left the restaurant. Haskell Sims was still in discussion with the older gentleman.

"I would like to join you one of these nights," Millie said. "With Joe's and Vaughn's permission, of course."

"I will ask them," Betsey promised.

They parted ways at the hotel, and Betsey went to her room, where she spent several hours reading up on séances again and Nina knitted.

After a couple of hours, she put her book aside. The wind was rattling her window, and she suspected they would have a storm tonight, if not sooner.

She grabbed a shawl, told Nina where she was headed, and went downstairs, intending to see Joe. Nina jumped up and scampered after her. As they walked towards the cabinetry shop, they passed several people she didn't know, but most nodded and smiled as they scurried by. The townspeople here were a friendly bunch, Betsey thought. She relaxed as they walked.

Wind whipped at her shawl as she crossed to the shop. She could hear voices inside.

"Well, it might be a good idea to make another

display piece with a similar design," Vaughn was saying as she entered the shop, Nina behind her.

"Yes, but for how much?" Joe asked.

As she approached, they both straightened up.

****

Betsey Chalmers was a beautiful woman. Not just pretty, with her dark blonde curls and blue-gray eyes. But her smile and the positive, bubbly outlook of her inner self added to the beauty of the woman.

She was spirited enough to be interesting, not some dull person. She seemed like an innocent, but he would bet his boots that with the right man, she would be a passionate lover. She seemed kind and sweet and would probably make a loyal wife and good mother—

He stopped. Why was he thinking like this? He would never be the one to marry a good woman like Betsey Chalmers. Not a half-breed like him—

Vaughn swallowed.

"How can we help you?" he asked in a cool voice.

"I need to speak to Joe," she answered.

Joe moved closer, turning pale. "Violet? The baby?"

"There's no news yet," she assured him. She glanced at Vaughn. "Can you speak to me for a few minutes, cousin?"

"Of course." He wiped his hands on a rag.

Leaving Vaughn wondering what was going on as she whispered to his business partner.

Betsey and her timid maid left shortly afterwards, including him in their goodbyes.

"What was that all about?" he asked his friend and business partner. "And aren't you supposed to ride out with her this afternoon?"

Joe shook his head. "It's blowing up out there. I expect it will storm soon. We agreed to go another day." He glanced at the window, through which a strong wind was gusting. He turned back to Vaughn. "I slipped and said something to Millie last week about the séances. And now she wants to talk to Betsey about them. Betsey felt it wasn't her place to discuss them without my—our permission. I told her it would be all right. Is that okay with you?" Joe looked faintly embarrassed.

"Yeah," Vaughn said. "If you want to pursue this odd way of collecting information, you can share it with her." He knew how sweet Joe was on Millie. "Just warn her not to talk to anyone else," he finished, frowning. The last thing he wanted was for all the townspeople to know their search was continuing. He didn't want them calling attention to themselves.

"I already told her mum's the word," Joe assured him. "Thanks, Vaughn. Also, she wants to join us one night." He hesitated, then asked casually, "What do you think of Betsey?"

"She seems nice enough," Vaughn replied shortly,

Joe raised his eyebrows. "That's all you have to say?"

"Yes."

Joe looked disappointed in his response. He hesitated, as if he wanted to say more.

"Let's get back to work," Vaughn suggested, and they did.

****

Betsey lit the candles as wind gusted through the open window.

Although it wasn't eight o'clock yet, the lowering

clouds were making everything nearly dark outside. With the wind whipping up, she'd seen people scurrying down the street, going home, getting their horses in the livery or their own barns, and calling to their children and dogs. They were in for a storm for certain, but the area could use the rain that was coming, so most people were quite happy, she guessed. The last few weeks had been dry, Joe had told her. Rivers would fill up, and dry creeks would run once again, if they got a substantial rain.

She'd have to close the windows farther, before the wind blew out the candles. Or use only the oil lamp, but that was flickering in the gusts of wind, too.

She knew from experience that spirits often were more apt to come through during a lightning storm, although her cousin Drew didn't know why. He had theories on this, of course. The electric currents in the air might attract them, he surmised; or perhaps the flashes of lightning simply made it easier to see the spirits who were there. No matter. Whatever it was, she sincerely hoped tonight's storm would bring at least one spirit.

She was hoping to call forth Red Feather, an Indian spirit who often had come through to them in the past. He had helped them in their quest to contact others.

She went to the window and looked out. The street was deserted now. But as she watched, Sally and her mother came out of the restaurant, shut, and locked the door, and then, linking arms, hurried down the street. When they came to the corner, they turned left. Betsey watched them until they were out of sight. She knew they lived nearby and would be home within moments. She guessed that with the approaching storm, they'd decided to close a little earlier than usual.

Movement caught her eyes. Vaughn and Joe were walking down the street, approaching the hotel. Joe was waving his hands in an animated manner, and Vaughn was shaking his head. What were they discussing? she wondered. Were they debating the use of her séances? She hoped Vaughn would be convinced after a few sessions that it was a legitimate way to gather information.

She moved away from the window, and went to check on the candles, the lamp, and the items she'd left on a side table—a small drum and a stick. In the past, her cousin Drew had left a trumpet belonging to a family member on a sideboard, and a few times, spirits had made use of it. She hadn't brought the trumpet along—it was too bulky and being that it was a family heirloom, Drew preferred to keep it at home—but she had brought a small drum with her. She wanted to try making use of it now.

"We'll be starting soon," she called to Nina. She'd left the bedroom door and windows open so the air could keep the rooms cooler. But now she closed them part of the way.

She reflected on her conversation with Joe that afternoon. He'd admitted he had told Millie about their experiments, as he called them. He wanted the gold so he would be a rich man, not for himself; but to provide well for Millie. And he had blurted that declaration out to Millie just a week ago.

He'd had the grace to look apologetic. "I'm sorry, Betsey," he'd said. "I should have kept the secret. But I was so eager to tell Millie what I hoped—"

"It's all right, Joe. How do you and Vaughn feel

about her joining us for a séance?" Betsey had asked.

"I'd like it. I'll talk to Vaughn, but I think he won't care one way or the other," he had said.

A knocking on the door now interrupted her thoughts, alerting her that the two men had arrived. She opened it, smiling. "Good evening."

"Hi," Joe said.

"Evening," Vaughn muttered.

His mouth was in a straight line, and he looked reluctant to be here, Betsey observed. She turned to Joe. "I am going to try to reach Red Feather, an Indian guide who has helped us before."

Joe nodded, looking intrigued. "Violet mentioned him in her letters."

Vaughn raised his eyebrows. "An Indian guide?"

"Many times, spirit guides come forward to help mediums during their quests to contact other spirits," Betsey told him. "It is not uncommon to have an Indian guide."

"What tribe he is from? Originally?"

Betsey thought it was a good question, though an unusual one. Only Violet had ever asked that question.

"He told us he was a Lenape Indian, from Drew's area of New Jersey," Betsey answered. "Do you know much about them?"

Vaughn's answer was a snort. "No. Not about the Lenape. Except they were a farming tribe, I believe."

His interest and the way he answered her one question made Betsey think that he might not know about the Lenape tribe, but he did have some knowledge about Indians. Perhaps knowledge of those here out west.

The two men, Betsey, and Nina took their places

around the table. The room was darkening, as the skies outside grew black. Wind whisked through the windows, which she'd left only slightly open, lifting the edge of the curtains. The candles flickered.

"We have come together to call forth the spirits of those departed," Betsey began after a moment of silence. "We seek to communicate." She paused, then went on. "We ask for a guide to help us with our search. Red Feather, you have guided us before. Can you come forward and help us?"

There was silence. Then, a feeling of heaviness grew in the air, as if a body had displaced some of it.

"Who joins us?" she whispered.

A deep male voice answered, "It is I, Red Feather."

Red Feather! She had succeeded in contacting him! Her heart beat rapidly. "Thank you, Red Father," she said. "We seek to contact the spirits of The Spaniard, Carlos Ayala, or his friend, Pedro Martinez. Can you help us?"

At least five minutes went by.

Betsey waited, hardly daring to breathe, to see if Red Feather could help them. Joey clutched her hand tightly. Vaughn's was firm around hers, but she noticed the skeptical expression on his face. Nina sat on the other side of the table, looking scared.

Lightning lit up the room, followed by a burst of thunder.

"They are not available presently," Red Feather announced suddenly. "But, another wants to come through."

Betsey inclined her head. "By all means."

A young man's voice spoke up, near Vaughn's shoulder. "Vaughn, it is I!"

Vaughn startled, his face turning white in the dark "Victor!" he exclaimed.

Chapter 7

"Yes, it is me, brother," the voice replied firmly.

Betsey stared by Vaughn's shoulder, where the voice had emanated from. Excitement bubbled up in her. She tightened her hand in his.

Nina gave a startled cry.

"Welcome, Victor," Betsey said, striving to sound calm though her heart beat rapidly at his words. She could feel perspiration gathering on her brow.

"Welcome," Joe echoed, looking surprised but pleased.

"Victor." Vaughn's voice shook. He paused, then said, "I have missed you every day, Vic."

"And I you. But it is grand here. I only came back now to warn you."

"Warn me?"

Betsey bent forward. Warn Vaughn of what? She wanted to speak but thought Vaughn should carry the conversation now, since this was his sibling. Her hand trembled with a mixture of awe and trepidation.

"Of danger. There are those—" Victor's voice became garbled suddenly.

"Yes?" she urged quietly.

"Those who would—try to thwart you in your quest."

Vaughn frowned. "Who?"

The next sentence was so garbled that Betsey could

54

not make out the words, except for "men."

"Can you repeat that?" she asked, leaning forward as wind gusted again.

"—those men." It sounded like Victor was having trouble getting through. "Want to—warn you—"

Lightning lit up the room again. The boom that followed shook the hotel building.

Nina gasped.

And for a moment, the outline of a man showed in the flare of light. He extended his arm towards them. "—danger—" was the only distinct word Betsey could make out.

Then, his image was gone. A popping sound followed instantly.

This time Joe gasped, and Betsey knew her own mouth was hanging open.

Vaughn looked stunned.

"God damn," Joe whispered. Then, as if realizing she and Nina were nearby, he said, "Sorry, ladies."

Vaughn whispered, "You said it, Joe."

Betsey, attempting to control the séance, spoke firmly. "Victor, are you still present?"

There was no response.

She tried again. "Red Feather, are you with us?"

Again, they were met with silence, except for the sound of the escalating storm.

She sat back. "I believe we will not hear from anyone else this night. Perhaps the turbulent storm has severed our connection to the spirit world."

"But what a response!" Joe's eyes were shining in the darkness. "We reached Red Feather and your brother." He dropped Betsey's hand and clutched at Vaughn's.

"My brother," Vaughn whispered, still looking like he could barely believe it. Stunned and—a little awestruck.

"Did you recognize his voice?" Betsey asked in her most gentle voice.

Vaughn swallowed. "Yes," he whispered. "And—when we saw him in the flash of light—his voice dwindled. "I could-I could swear that was him."

Betsey placed her hand on his arm, recognizing the man's disbelief and confusion. "The first time you see or hear a loved one, it can be difficult," she said, keeping her voice soothing. "I remember when we first heard my Aunt Claire. And I hope—" she glanced at Joe—"that someday I will make contact with my own dear mother."

Vaughn stood up abruptly and went to peer out the window.

"Let me talk to him," Joe whispered to Betsey. He stood and went over to Vaughn, placing a hand on his friend's shoulder. "Kind of a shock, ain't it?" he asked, his tone kind.

"I wouldn't have believed it without seeing—and hearing it—with my own eyes and ears," Vaughn stated. "I still can't—" he swung around to stare at Betsey. "I can barely believe it."

Nina sat silent, her eyes wide. Betsey could see her hands shaking.

"It is hard, the first time," Betsey said, making her voice calm and smooth. She stood also and came up to the two men. "It takes some getting used to."

"But it's exciting," Joe pressed on. "This means we really might be able to contact The Spaniard!"

Vaughn gave his friend a dubious look but said

nothing.

"It is certainly possible!" Betsey affirmed. "During separate nights, we have contacted three different individuals—Eddie O'Roarke, Red Feather, and now Vaughn's brother, Victor Montgomery.

"In my experience, it's not good to do séances every night in a row. We should take a break." Betsey continued. "We need a rest, and the spirits may, as well. So, perhaps we will skip tomorrow but try again later in the week—on Friday?"

"Sounds good to me," Joe said.

Vaughn shrugged. "The spirits tire?"

"We don't know, but the humans do," she pointed out.

"I am going to bed," Nina announced, standing abruptly. She was shaking as she left the room.

"Vaughn says he doesn't mind if Millie joins us," Joe added.

"Will she have trouble with her parents if she does?" Betsey questioned.

Joe grinned. "We thought about that already. I spoke to her a few hours ago. She's simply going to say that she's coming here to visit with you. I don't think they'll object. Her mother was impressed when she heard you come from New York society."

"That's fine," Betsey said. New York society? Maybe, but she had tired of the whirlwind of social life there. The artificial gaiety of parties and the constant talk of fashions among the society ladies. She much preferred the quieter lives and the town of her cousins Drew and Violet.

Vaughn was staring at Betsey now, watching her. Was he put off by the idea that she was a so-called society woman? she wondered. She wasn't really a true society lady. Unlike some of her friends, she didn't want to spend all her time attending parties, talking about fashion, and looking for future husbands. She liked to read, travel, and enjoyed spending time with her family above all.

The men departed a few minutes later, Vaughn still wearing an expression of shock. Betsey sat down immediately to make notes, then added more information to the new letter to Violet and Drew she was writing, detailing the night's activities. She decided to post the letter tomorrow.

She went to check on Nina, who had looked scared. She was lying in bed "Are you all right?" she whispered, just in case her maid was asleep.

"No," was Nina's answer. "Oh, miss! I don't think we should be contacting the souls of those who've passed. It's—it's not right."

"It has never hurt us in any way," she tried to reassure the woman. "We have done it at my cousin Drew's house many times."

"But it could be dangerous now," Nina said.

"It's good for us to know if Joe and Vaughn are in danger," she said. "And, Nina, if you don't want to attend another séance, I will not force you to." She nibbled on her lip. So far she had been so excited by Victor Montgomery's appearance she hadn't given thought to the danger that he spoke about, but forewarned was forearmed.

"I don't want to!" Nina wailed, sounding like a scared child.

Betsey sighed. "Of course I will not force you."

That seemed to mollify the maid. Betsey returned

to the main room, where she watched the storm from the window. The thunder and lightning had abated, leaving a steady, welcome rain. After a half hour, she too got ready for bed.

Sleep eluded her for a while. Between the excitement of the séance and the revelation of Joe's feelings for Millie, she had a lot to think about. Finally, the steady beat of the rain soothed her enough to go to sleep.

Her last thought was to wonder what Vaughn was thinking, right now, this very minute…

****

If the rain had stopped, Vaughn would have saddled his horse and gone for a night ride, something he often enjoyed doing. But there was no sense in getting soaked. So when Joe indicated he was going to turn in, Vaughn said he just wanted to check the cabinet shop, wanting some time alone.

The familiar smell of cut wood and chips greeted him when he entered.

Everything was fine.

But he was too restless to go to bed. His thoughts tumbled about. The séance. His brother.

He walked around the large room, slowly. After a few minutes, he checked the locks, circling the room again, then went upstairs to the apartment he shared with Joe.

He walked into the small parlor. There was a generously sized kitchen in the back. Off to the side were two small bedrooms. Joe's door was partly ajar, and a small lamp was on. He knew his friend liked to read in bed, so he walked quietly to his own room, opened the door, and went inside.

He could not get his brother and the séance out of his mind. He sat in an armchair, staring out the window at the rain streaming down.

Victor. Victor, who had passed on some six years ago.

He still missed his brother terribly. It was as if there was a big hole on his insides, a hole where Victor used to be.

Victor had never been the healthiest child, but he'd grown up to be a serious, well-intentioned adult. He'd wanted to have a home, a family—but the girl he'd cared for deeply, Abbie, had turned him down and married another man. A man from a fine, upstanding family. Not like the Montgomery family. Victor had been crushed.

It had also given Vaughn one more reason to decide that marriage and a family were not in the cards for him.

****

Betsey posted her letter the following morning, then got busy going over her notes on the seance to see if she'd left anything out. She hadn't. Since the air was cool from the rain last night, she decided to go for a long walk. Nina accompanied her.

They explored the side streets of the town and were walking down one when Millie came out of a stately looking white house that was larger than its neighbors.

"Hello!" Betsey greeted the woman. She drew closer. "Do you want to stroll about with us??"

"Delighted to!" Millie responded, linking her arm with Betsey's. Betsey caught the scent of lavender from her friend. Perhaps she had lavender sachets in her clothes.

They strolled down one street, then another. Millie pointed out the boarding house, a large home owned by the banker, and a large home owned by another well-to-do family, the Lewises.

"I really don't like Ramona Lewis," Millie confided. "She's so stuck up. "Just because she's beautiful, she looks down her nose at everyone else in town."

"I don't care for people like that, either," Betsey murmured, as Nina followed them. "I did meet her the other day, and she was not friendly."

They approached the Montgomery & Moore Carpenters and Cabinet Makers Shoppe.

"The sign for the business is beautiful," Betsey observed, noting the fancy lettering and design featuring curlicues and furniture.

"It was made by Rosemary and her daughter, Flora," Millie said. "They've made a lot of signs hereabouts. And they decorate coffins, too."

"Really? How surprising!" Betsey said.

Millie laughed. "Rosemary's husband is the undertaker here in Wylder. Decorating coffins was how she got her start in the signage business. Lots of stores and places have signs made by her, and now her daughter helps, too. She inherited her mother's talent."

Betsey smiled, enjoying her tour of the quaint town, which reminded her of Twin Bridges, the town where her cousins Drew and Violet resided. Of course, being out west, Wylder was less modern than the northeast area of America. And Drew's house was a mansion compared to even the larger homes here.

She told Millie a little about her family, describing her two older brothers, losing her father years ago and now her mother, and about her favorite cousins, Drew and his sister, Mary. And about Drew meeting Violet, since she was his assistant for his séance work and research. She told her new friend about Drew and Mary's brother Charles, and how he had been murdered, and how their séances had helped bring the killer to justice. She paused, taking a breath as they reached the edge of town.

Millie's eyes grew round as Betsey spoke. "Oh, goodness, how horrible! Murdered! But how exciting that you helped catch the culprit!"

"Yes. It was Drew's fondest wish to see justice done, since Charles' untimely death," Betsey said.

"How wonderful that they caught the perpetrator," Millie continued. "I hope he went to jail for a long time."

"It was a woman." Betsey grimaced. "Horrible, really, to know a woman could be guilty of such a heinous crime as planning a murder."

They walked in silence for a minute back the way they'd come. Nina, who'd heard these stories from Betsey as they traveled together out West, was silent.

"Joe said that you want to find The Spaniard, the man who discovered the gold mine that has become legendary," Millie said in a low voice, glancing to see no one else was nearby. "And you haven't contacted him yet but have had a small success with someone else."

"That is true." Betsey did not feel comfortable sharing that Vaughn's brother had come through last night, since that was highly personal. Although she could share about Mr. O'Roarke. Betsey glanced at her new friend. She could see hope shining in Millie's eyes.

She wanted to groan. Joe had shared his hopes and dreams with Millie, she knew. The hope that he would find the mine, become a wealthy man, be able to provide for Millie in an opulent manner, and thus be accepted as her husband by Millie's family. But what if he didn't find it? Betsey felt the pressure to help him.

"So far we have not reached anyone who can help with our quest." Betsey stated it plainly, not wishing to raise Millie's hopes to too high a level. If she loved Joe for himself, that was most important! In fact, she fervently hoped that Millie did. Joe deserved more than a wife who only cared about material possessions.

It was as if Millie read her thoughts. "I don't care about riches," she stated. "I would be content with Joe as he is, a skilled carpenter and cabinet-maker."

"That's good," Betsey said. She smiled at her friend.

Millie whispered, "He said I might join you in a séance."

"I know," Betsey whispered back. "We will be conducting one on Friday evening. Do you want to come then?"

"I'd love to!" she gushed, clasping her hands. Then, lowering her voice, she continued, "I will tell my folks I am going to visit with you that evening. I don't think they'll object, despite your being Joe's cousin. They don't think he's good enough or rich enough for me. But," she added, "My mother is impressed that you come from a New York City family. She says she can tell by your clothes and the way you carry yourself that you are a young lady of quality, as she put it." She smiled at Betsey.

Betsey couldn't help a laugh. "If she knew I was

leading séances, she might not say that."

"True." Millie grinned. She stepped closer to Betsey. "I can't wait for Friday."

****

The following day, Betsey had her chance to practice her gun shooting. Joe sent a note around with Leon, his young helper, that he would have time in the afternoon to practice with her and Nina.

She and Nina met Joe at the cabinetry shoppe, and they walked to the edge of town where Joe announced many people practiced. There was a low fence, and he lined up some tin cans there and demonstrated the proper stance to use when shooting. Betsey tried, and she was able to nick two of the five cans on her first round and shoot another one off completely.

"Very good," Joe told her. "Your stance is excellent, Cousin. Remember to aim and hold your breath, keeping your arm in position. Try it again and then we'll give Nina a turn."

This time Betsey hit four cans, again knocking one down completely. "I used to practice with my brothers," she said,

"Very good!" he praised. "You're doing well, Betsey. Now you try," he said to Nina.

"I've only had one lesson, from Betsey's oldest brother, when he heard we were coming out here," Nina admitted.

Joe had to correct her posture. On her first attempt, Nina only nicked one can. He helped her hold the gun, and she nicked two on the second round. But on her third attempt, she nicked three.

"You're getting better!" Joe praised.

Nina looked pleased, Betsey thought. This would

be good for her. She'd had so many fears about the dangers of the West when they came out here. Betsey had had to ignore them. She'd reminded her maid again and again that New York City could be a dangerous place, as could any city, even London.

Joe wanted Betsey to try shooting again, and she successfully nicked all five cans—one of them hard enough to fall over. Nina tried again and nicked three and toppled two.

"You two are doing very well!" Joe said. "Next time you'll practice with Vaughn, and I don't believe you'll need many lessons."

"I feel comfortable holding a gun, Cousin." Betsey smiled at Joe.

****

Friday dawned bright and clear and warmer than the previous two days. Betsey heard the hotel staff muttering about storms coming again later, although they seemed happy about the idea of more rain. Joe took her for a ride out to the lake, and she was feeling more confident that she knew the location and how to get there.

Joe was quiet on the ride, seeming to be in an introspective mood. They lapsed into silence often. Betsey tried asking him about Vaughn several times, but he seemed unwilling to talk about his business partner except to answer a few casual questions. They didn't stay out long, as Joe said they'd gotten a big order yesterday, and they were busy creating a custom bedroom set.

When she returned to the hotel, Betsey saw maids busily dusting.

"The creeks are still low," a young girl said to

another as she cleaned the hotel's parlor area.

"We do need more rain," the other answered. "But, I hope it is clear Saturday for the dance."

By evening, clouds had overtaken the sky. Perhaps another thunderstorm would help with contacting the spirits, Betsey thought, as she prepared the room. She set out the candles, the drum, and brought an extra chair over to the round table.

The first knock on her door heralded the arrival of Millie, looking flushed and eager. "I'm so excited! Imagine, we could hear—or even see—a ghost! Is it scary? Oh dear, I hope I shan't faint. Oh, no, listen to me, I'm practically babbling," she went on.

Betsey grinned. "I remember how excited I was for my first séance. No, I'm sure you won't faint. The only one who ever fainted at our séances was someone who was guilty and was afraid a spirit would reveal that."

"Oh my!" Millie's eyes grew rounder.

Nina still insisted she didn't want to join them, so she'd retreated to the bedroom.

Another knock sounded, and Betsey let Vaughn and Joe in.

Joe looked decidedly pleased to see Millie. Vaughn, not so much.

They gathered around the table and sat after Betsey lit the candles and lowered the light on the oil lamp. "Let us hold hands," she directed, and they did. Millie was on her left, and Joe on Millie's left. Vaughn was on Betsey's right.

"We ask for spirits who are able to come through," she said quietly. "We seek to speak with The Spaniard, Carlos Ayala, or his friend, Pedro Martinez."

There was silence. After five minutes, Betsey

asked, "Red Feather, can you help us in our journey? We seek The Spaniard or his friend."

"One wishes to speak," Red Feather said in his somber, ghostly voice. Betsey felt Millie start at the sound.

"*Me llamo*—it is I, Pedro," a heavily accented voice said.

Instantly Millie's hand tightened in hers. Vaughn sat up straighter.

"Pedro, thank you for joining us," Betsey said smoothly. "*Muchas gracias*. We are seeking the mine your friend, The Spaniard, found, the gold mine. We would like to find it—and of course, give him and you all due credit for finding it first."

"He always dreamed that a museum would be established there and named for him," Pedro said. "And for me, too."

"We can do that," Joe assured the spirit. "When we find it, we will establish a museum there in both your names."

"*Muy bien*, very good," Pedro said. His voice came from closer to Joe's shoulder, as if he was moving about the room. "And help the orphaned children who live at the Mission nearby. *Esta cerca de*—" and his words became jumbled.

Betsey could speak some French, but only a little Spanish. She raised her eyebrows.

Millie jumped in. "I understand him. He says it is near the foothills of the mountains," she translated.

"The foothills of the Medicine Bow Mountains?" For the first time, Vaughn spoke.

"*Sí, sí*," Pedro answered. "But Carlos also buried a map not far from this town."

"Do you know where?" Joe asked. "Where the map is, I mean?"

There was a moment of silence. "I will ask," came the answer.

"Perhaps The Spaniard might join us?" Betsey asked.

There was a chuckle. "With two such beautiful ladies here, I believe he will," Pedro stated. "It is his hope that one of these days someone will find the mine. And establish a museum and give some of the money to the orphans in the mission near Wylder, where The Spaniard used to visit. He liked the church and the Padre there very much."

"We will do that," Joe said solemnly. "I swear it."

"I will ask him…" Pedro's voice was beginning to fade. He said something in Spanish again.

Lightning flashed in the room. There was no outline of a human being, but Pedro's voice came through clearly immediately afterward.

"I am in touch with him here…I will tell him what you said."

Thunder rumbled.

"We do appreciate that," Betsey said, and there were murmurs all around the table.

"Goodbye, *amigos*…" the voice was fading again. "*Hasta la vista*…"

Wind blew into the room suddenly from the open window.

The candles flickered. The group sat still, but there was no more contact with Pedro.

They waited several minutes to see if he returned.

Three minutes later, Joe sighed. "I guess that's it for this evening."

"Well." Betsey smiled. "I would say that was a successful séance."

"Oh yes! It was!" Millie exclaimed.

Joe was nodding, and Betsey turned to Vaughn. "What did you think?" She couldn't quite keep the challenging note from her voice.

He sighed. "It appears genuine."

"Indeed it does!" Millie declared robustly. She focused on Betsey. "Do you think Pedro will return with the Spaniard another night? And tell us where the map is or describe the location of the mine?"

"We can only hope," Betsey said. She smiled and asked, "What did he say in Spanish near the end?"

"Something about his friend coming another time to visit," Millie said.

Joe sat back. "That would be ideal."

Joe's face lit up with hope. Millie's was, too.

Betsey fervently hoped it would happen.

"When can we have another séance?" Joe asked eagerly.

"Tomorrow is the social," Millie reminded him.

"I know." He smiled at her. "Never fear, I won't miss it."

"Sunday?" Betsey asked.

Millie looked crestfallen. "My parents like to spend Sunday with family, after church. They won't let me come back here then. And they have invited another family to join us."

"Monday, Mr. Watson is coming to the shop. He wants to order furniture for his new home, a lot of it. And he's offered to take us out for dinner and to the saloon," Vaughn said.

"So let's plan on Tuesday," Betsey suggested.

Millie and Joe said "yes" simultaneously. Vaughn nodded.

"Can I walk you home?" Joe asked Millie.

She smiled. "Of course."

Betsey said good night to the two, and they left her suite. Vaughn started towards the door, then turned back.

"That was—interesting," he said slowly.

"I hope these séances have convinced you that there is life after death, and given the right circumstances, we can make contact with some spirits," Betsey said. Idly, she picked up the drum, then set it down on the sideboard, where it rattled.

"Maybe," he said, his expression revealing none of his thoughts. "Goodnight, Miz Chalmers."

"Betsey," she corrected automatically.

"Betsey," he whispered the word, but it sounded different than his other spoken words. More…personal.

More intimate.

A shiver swept up her spine.

****

The day of the social dawned bright and clear, and last night's rain had lowered the temperatures. As Betsey strolled down the main street of town with Nina after breakfast, she looked forward to a comfortable day without the intense, dry heat she had encountered sometimes in the past weeks as she traveled west.

She had taken to bringing a parasol to shield her from the worst of the sun's strong rays during the afternoon; but in the morning, she liked to walk with the sun touching her face. She knew she now had a few freckles, but she also had a healthy glow to her skin which she liked.

She was looking forward to the social with great anticipation. She imagined it was less formal than the balls in New York City and even the ones held in neighboring New Jersey. But Millie had told her there would be live music and plenty of refreshments. All the townspeople would be there, including "loads of eligible men and women" as her friend put it. In that way, it sounded similar to balls that Betsey had attended in the past.

She and Nina ran into Millie after they began their walk, and Betsey invited her to join them as they promenaded in town.

As they strolled down the main street, the sheriff passed them and tipped his hat. She'd met him a few days ago while she was walking with Nina. So far, Betsey hadn't observed any crime in this small town, although she had heard from the gossipy hotel staff that a man was caught trying to steal another man's horse, and had been thrown in jail; he could be hanged for such an offense, Joe had told her. Plus, her cousin had said there were usually a couple of drunks in jail every weekend when they were spending their money and got into fights.

"His deputy is young and handsome," Millie said a few minutes later. "If I wasn't so interested in Joe…"

Betsey laughed at Millie's matchmaking attempt. "I suppose when I go back to New York City, I may seriously look for a husband. My mother was always saying it was past time, since I am in my mid-twenties now."

"You're not so old," Millie declared. "I am twenty, and my parents are always pressuring me to get married."

Betsey smiled. She'd never felt that she had to snare a husband, the way many young women in the city did; but she'd admitted to herself it would be nice to have someone to love who loved her in return. Like Drew and Violet. Now, there was a love match.

"It will have to be a love match," Betsey told her friend. "I don't want a simple arrangement. My parents left me enough money that I don't have to rush to get married."

Millie nodded her head vigorously. "For me, it is the same. Mama and Father want me to make a good match; but I could never marry a man simply because it would provide me with a nice house and comfortable life." She sighed. "I wish they would understand that."

"Was theirs a marriage arranged by families?" Betsey asked, curious.

"In a way. They both grew up in Illinois and knew each other's families since they were very young. Mama said it was always assumed they would marry, and they went along with it. Both families were old and wealthy, so Mama considered it a good match. But— they hold only a little affection for each other, I think." Millie frowned.

"Oh, that is too bad," Betsey murmured. "My parents were very fond of each other. That's what I want. And my brothers, too, married women they cared deeply for."

"How nice." Millie sounded wistful.

They continued to walk down the street, until Millie excused herself to go primp for the party

Betsey and Nina returned to the hotel, walking slowly, and once there, Betsey sat down to read. She paused for lunch, but there would be food at the party, which started at seven o'clock, so she ate lightly.

Nina helped her do her hair, sweeping it up but leaving some tendrils to escape. Betsey had left her curling iron at home, thinking she was in Wylder only to help Joe and Vaughn. She hadn't anticipated a social life.

As the hour of the social drew near, she put on the best dress she'd brought with her, her dark blue with gold trim. She had brought no jewelry on her trip, afraid she'd lose something or have anything valuable robbed on her journey. But she did have a pretty gold shawl, which she arranged around her shoulders, and a matching gold bow which she put in her hair.

Joe had offered to escort them to the party, so she and Nina went downstairs to wait for him. Joe had informed her that in this area, servants were treated better than in the East and often joined in on festivities.

To her surprise, as she came down the stairs, the door to the hotel opened, and Vaughn strode in.

She stopped on the stairs. He looked so handsome, dressed in a jacket, a nice cream-colored shirt, and a western-style tie, his hair neatly combed, and his hat dust-free. She caught her breath, appreciating his broad shoulders, tall stature, and dark good looks. His usual serious expression changed into a smile when he caught sight of her. He whipped off his hat and bowed.

Slowly, she descended the rest of the stairs, her heartbeat accelerating.

"You look very pretty." His whispered words sent a shot of warmth to her heart.

"Thank you." She smiled at him. "I'm glad to see you. Is Joe coming, too?"

Vaughn shook his head. "He's waiting at the

Brown's barn for Millie to arrive so he can claim the first dance with her."

Betsey grinned. "They really are sweet on each other."

Nina joined them.

"Yes, they are." He offered Betsey his arm, and she took it. Offering the other arm to Nina, the three proceeded out of the hotel and onto the street. The air was warm, but not overly so, and a breeze kept it delightful.

"It's too bad Millie's parents are trying to push a match with an older man," Betsey said as they walked. "Joe really would make Millie a good husband. He's nice and loyal."

"And one of the hardest-working men I ever met," Vaughn said, nodding.

"Yes," she agreed. "I just don't understand…" her voice dwindled.

Vaughn grimaced. "Most families want to make a good match for their daughters." A shadow passed over his face, then was gone. She wondered what had caused that dark look.

"Some people marry for love. My parents did. So did my cousin Drew, who married Joe's sister," Betsey said spiritedly as they tread on the wooden sidewalk, their footsteps making a rhythmic clatter. "I have rarely seen a couple who are so devoted as Drew and Violet."

Vaughn looked like he didn't quite believe her words, with his brow furrowed, his mouth a straight line. As they approached the Brown home on the outskirts of town, they could hear fiddlers tuning up in a barn behind the house. She noted that people were entering the barn, smiling and laughing, dressed in their

Sunday best for the party.

Vaughn led them into the building, and Betsey spotted Joe talking to Millie and another woman and man about their age. Nearby, Millie's mother and an older man who must be her father stood by, chatting with a gray-haired couple. Millie's mother was looking over at Joe, though, and frowning.

Betsey sighed inwardly.

Nina saw someone from the hotel staff whom she had gotten friendly with and excused herself to talk to her.

The fiddlers struck up a tune. Vaughn turned to her. "May I have this dance?" he asked in formal tones.

"I'd love to!" Betsey declared.

He placed his arm around her waist and took her hand with his other one, and they swung onto the dance floor, closely followed by several other couples, including Joe and Millie.

Vaughn seemed to have a natural sense of rhythm, and Betsey found it easy to follow his lead. They stepped together in time to the bright music, as many couples crowded the dance floor. His hand on her waist was warm, even through the fabric of her dress; the hand holding hers was rough but held her hand comfortably. As if her hand was made to be nestled there. She could smell sandalwood soap on him, and she saw close up that his hair had been tamed with some kind of tonic. His usual serious face looked lighter, more carefree than usual, as they danced.

She smiled up at Vaughn. He gazed down at her, and his answering smile lightened her heart. She felt like she was floating, swaying with the stars in the darkening sky outside.

Another couple bumped into them, interrupting her reverie.

"Sorry," the stout man mumbled, moving away.

Vaughn's smile faded, as if he was brought back to reality.

But Betsey continued to smile up at him. She was enjoying the dance thoroughly, enjoying being with him held in his arms. It felt surprisingly delightful.

The music ended, and Vaughn stepped back, giving a quick bow.

"Thank you, Miz Betsey."

Still so formal. She sighed inwardly, feeling like she had come plopping down from the heavenly heights where she had been floating.

"I enjoyed the dance," she said.

"Would you like something cool to drink?" he offered.

"Perhaps later," she answered. "Thank you." She inclined her head.

At that moment, Haskell Sims appeared at her elbow. "Good evening, Miss Chalmers," he said in his Southern drawl. "May I have this next dance?"

She turned to regard him. He looked handsome and rather debonair in his clothes, a jacket and waistcoat and tie which were more formal than what most of the other men were wearing tonight. His light brown hair was slicked back, and he still looked like a gambler, although he wore more formal attire than he usually did. He resembled many of the men she had seen immersed in poker games as she traveled west.

"Yes," she agreed, and he led her back to the dance floor.

Vaughn, meanwhile, turned and disappeared into

the crowd.

"You look very fetching tonight, Miz Chalmers," Haskell said.

"Please, call me Betsey. Perhaps I can meet your sister tonight," she suggested as they began to move around the dance floor.

Nina danced by with a young man Betsey had seen at the telegraph office.

"She would be happy to meet you, I'm sure" Haskell said, steering her expertly.

Haskell Sims was a smooth dancer, and she guessed he had danced in many ballrooms throughout America. Perhaps in Europe, too.

"I get the feeling you have traveled, and danced, extensively," Betsey said. "You are quite accomplished."

He nodded his head, smiling. "I do enjoy dancing. And I have spent time from Chicago to New Orleans, which is my favorite city."

"Have you gambled there, too?" she asked.

His smile deepened. "I have been known to gamble there—and win."

She'd been correct. "And Europe? Have you traveled there, as well?"

"Once to Paris. Although I would love to go back and see France again and visit England and other countries," he said as they moved in time to the music.

He held her a trifle tighter than necessary. Betsey didn't like it nearly as much as being held by Vaughn.

She moved so they were more separated. "Tell me about New Orleans. I've never been there."

He described lavish parties, men and women in stylish clothes, drinks flowing, and roulette wheels spinning. As the dance ended, he offered to get her a lemonade.

"Maybe later," Betsey said. She had enjoyed her dance with him. He was an interesting man. But she'd enjoyed her dance with Vaughn more.

"I'll take that as an invitation to claim you for another dance," Haskell said, bowing.

"Certainly. Now, I should find my friend Millie." She gave a swift curtsy and moved to search for her friend.

She found Millie talking to the milliner, and the three spoke for a few minutes before the sheriff asked Betsey to dance. After that she danced with the deputy, and then the mayor. She took a break, and the mayor brought her lemonade, and then Joe escorted her onto the dance floor.

They were partnered for the Virginia Reel, which was a really fun dance that Betsey had never done before. As they went through the turns, the caller instructed them what to do, and she was whirled around and went up and down the line with Joe. She had almost no time to talk to Joe, because the pace was fast and you changed partners during the dance.

"Now do-si-do your partner!" the caller instructed in a cheery voice.

Betsey found it was easy to follow the instructions and catch on to the steps, despite the fact that she'd never done this dance before.

She and Joe were both out of breath when they finished and stood on the sidelines, watching the next dance, a slower tune.

She felt very popular when a cowboy claimed her next, followed by Haskell Sims again.

The last few dances had been slower, and she had the opportunity to look at the lively crowd.

"Are you enjoying yourself, my dear?" Haskell asked, tilting his head toward hers.

"Very much." She smiled.

"I hope that you will take a buggy ride with me next week," he invited. "We can ride out to the lake, if you'd like." He must have sensed her hesitation, because he added, "My sister Louisa would like to join us. I will introduce you to her."

It might be a nice diversion. "Thank you, that would be nice," she answered, feeling relieved his sister would be along. Which surprised her. In New York, open carriage rides were often permitted without a chaperone, if one knew the gentleman. She'd think later about why she was so hesitant with Haskell.

"I hear tell that your cousin Joseph and Vaughn Montgomery are using some highly unusual methods to try to find the Spaniard's mine," Haskell said abruptly.

Surprise wound through Betsey. How had he heard that? She stared at him. "You should ask them," she said. "All I know is that they are trying to find the mine." Everyone seemed to know that, so she was not divulging anything secret.

"Everyone knows that." He echoed her thoughts. "Come now, my dear. I have heard they are actually trying to contact the spirit of the dead Spaniard to get information!" The music was loud, and she could barely hear his words. Fortunately, she doubted anyone else could hear them.

"Really?" she asked. How much could she safely tell him? Her cousin Drew had warned her against such men, telling her he'd heard many tales about gamblers, who were often sweet-talking men who frequented towns in the West and took advantage of the trusting people around them. "Where did you hear such a tale?" she asked Haskell.

"Don't play games," he snapped, then paused as they moved across the dance floor. "I am sorry," he said, his voice dropping. "I know you are involved, and I hoped you would be truthful with me."

She looked back at him, saying nothing.

Apparently, her silence made him uncomfortable. He frowned.

"Can you confirm that?" he asked, but his tone had grown softer.

She shook her head. She was not going to blab about their secret quest. "I'm afraid I don't know what you're talking about."

The dance ended. He regarded her for a moment, then sighed. "I see. Perhaps you have made a promise not to speak about this topic." He gave a somewhat stiff bow. "Please remember our plans to take a ride out to the lake."

She was sorry, now, that she had committed to spending time with him. She was afraid he would pester her with numerous questions. But she knew no way to gracefully avoid it, so she said, "I look forward to taking a short ride with you and your sister." Perhaps the addition of the word "short" would make him realize she could not be badgered into telling what she didn't want to. Plus, his sister would be along. Surely, she wouldn't want to follow this line of questions. Betsey glanced around. "Perhaps I could meet her now?"

"Of course. She's over by the punch bowl with the

mayor. I'll introduce you." He took her arm and led her over to a woman who was tall and had the same coloring as he did. Her features were somewhat plain, contrasted to Haskell's good looks.

"This is my sister, Louisa Sims," he said. "Louisa, Betsey Chalmers from New York City."

Louisa shook Betsey's hand enthusiastically. "I am so happy to meet you. New York! What brings you out here to Wylder?"

"Likewise," Betsey responded. "As far as Wylder, I wanted to do some traveling, and since my mother passed, I decided this was a good time. I came out west to visit my cousin, Joe Moore."

They chatted about the party, and then Vaughn approached. "May I have this dance?"

Betsey was relieved to walk onto the dance floor with him. Relieved to be away from Haskell Sims' questions and his prying eyes. Although his sister seemed nice enough.

And she was happy to move into Vaughn's arms for the dance. She concentrated on enjoying his company. As the fiddlers played a slower tune, she gazed at Vaughn.

Once again, she felt comfortable—more than comfortable—with him. She smiled up at him, thinking that his face, when he smiled, was just as handsome as the debonair Haskell Sims' face. Maybe Vaughn was even more so.

"Enjoying yourself?" Vaughn asked.

"Yes. Especially—" she decided to be frank— "when I dance with you."

He looked surprised. "I enjoy dancing with you, too," he responded. "But I should warn you about the man you just danced with, Haskell Sims."

"Warn me?"

"Yes. He is a renowned gambler."

"Oh, I do realize that."

"Well, do not let him encourage you into a card game or any games of chance. I don't trust him."

"I will be sure not to get into any games with him," she agreed.

She felt her cheeks flush, and not just from the heat in the large room, crowded with people.

"Betsey—would you like to go for a ride tomorrow?" He changed the topic. "Perhaps out to the lake again?"

It sure seemed like people around here considered that a romantic place. Which maybe it was.

But the suggestion, when it came from Haskell, did not leave her heart thumping. With Vaughn, it definitely did.

"I'd like that." She could barely contain her pleasure. She tried to look merely pleased and not joyous. Vaughn would wonder why the idea appealed to her so much.

His hand tightened on hers for a brief second.

She was tempted to tell him about Haskell's Sims' probing questions, but she didn't want to spoil the moment. Maybe it would be better to talk to Joe instead.

They continued to dance, silently, letting the music swirl around them. Betsey couldn't help smiling as she gazed into Vaughn's face. His answering smile warmed her to her toes.

When the dance ended, they were joined by Joe and Sally, a woman she had met briefly while strolling with Joe around town the week before. Sally and her mother owned a restaurant in Wylder. And then the mayor claimed a dance with Betsey again.

Then many of the women went to uncover the food on the long tables, so the music stopped as the musicians joined the lines to fill their plates. Betsey sat down across from Vaughn at a table, and she was soon introduced to a farmer, several cowboys, the town's doctor, and a saddle-maker, as well as a few of the women who lived nearby.

Throughout the evening, Betsey caught glimpses of Ramona Lewis looking beautiful, regal, and conceited. They spoke only briefly, with Ramona asking how she enjoyed this "little" social. "I guess it's not nearly as exciting as the parties in New York City which you are used to," she said.

"I'm enjoying myself very much!" Betsey declared. "I love dancing, and the folk dances here are so much fun! New York parties can be boring, I assure you."

Ramona gave her a look of disbelief.

Betsey enjoyed the late meal. When the dancing started again, Haskell Sims moved close by.

"May I have another dance?" he asked cordially.

She could think of no reason to decline. He was a good dancer, and an interesting man, even if his questions earlier had been probing. So she accepted.

As they moved on the dance floor, he said "My sister says that Monday in the early afternoon would be a good time for her to join us on the ride."

"That would be fine," Betsey agreed. Their next séance was not scheduled until Tuesday night. Joe had told her that for some reason, Mondays were usually busy at the shop, and she knew he and Vaughn were meeting with a client over dinner.

As Betsey danced with Haskell, she kept the topic to balls she had attended in New York, which seemed to interest the man, surprisingly. She gave him no chance to ask more questions, prattling on quite a bit. He did not try to stop her.

"I have heard that all the socialites and important families attend many formal balls in the great city," he remarked.

"That is true," she agreed, "And many of the hosts try to out-do each other. It gets absurd after a while with competitions for the decoration. And there are many people trying to marry off their eligible daughters." She wondered if Haskell might be considering a trip to the city to find a rich wife.

They whirled around the dance floor, and the dance ended.

"May I ask you for some punch?" Betsey requested politely. All this dancing was making her thirsty.

"Certainly," he replied and left her to get some.

She had a chance to watch those whirling by in the next dance before he returned. She saw Millie dancing with a young man she didn't know, and Joe with the milliner. And Vaughn passed with another woman she had seen about town, whose name she couldn't recall. She thought the woman worked in the general store.

"Here you are," Haskell said at her elbow, handing her the punch.

The announcer declared that the next song was to be the last of the night. Betsey hoped to be claimed by Vaughn, but Joe appeared and asked her to dance. She accepted, and Haskell looked disappointed, but she and

Joe went out to the dance floor as the fiddles started up.

"You don't want to dance with Millie?" she questioned him as Nina danced by with a man Betsey had seen her with earlier.

"I already danced with Millie four times," Joe said. "I don't want to make her parents mad." He swung her around.

Betsey caught sight of Millie with an older man. The man her parents had picked for her? she wondered. Haskell had also found a partner, someone Betsey didn't recognize.

The music ended. Everyone clapped and shouted.

"This was fun!" she declared to her "cousin."

"The dances usually are," he responded. "Come on, I'll walk you back. Millie's going back with her parents."

He took Betsey's arm. She found her shawl and wrapped it around her, assuming the night air would be cold compared to the crowded barn. They proceeded out the doors with a throng of people. She didn't see Vaughn among them.

"If you're looking for Vaughn, he's ahead, walking with a customer's daughter," Joe observed. "She's too young for him," he added.

Betsey could now see him ahead, with a red-haired young woman of about seventeen. She swallowed the spurt of jealousy she felt. She had no claim on Vaughn.

Still, she had been so happy in his arms! She told herself she'd examine those feelings later.

Joe insisted on walking her upstairs, not just to the hotel's door. "You never know when some drunken cowboys are lurking about," he said. "You can't be too careful."

"I appreciate that," she told him.

When she opened the door and discovered Nina had already arrived back, Joe took his leave. "See you soon."

After she'd locked the door behind him, Nina helped her to disrobe.

"Did you enjoy yourself?" she asked her maid.

"Oh, miss, it was so much fun!" the young woman replied.

"And did you dance with anyone who particularly caught your fancy?"

"Yes." She hesitated. "I did dance twice with Billy Sheehan, who works over at the telegraph office." She blushed after saying that.

Betsey smiled. She had seen the young man there and about town delivering missives. "That's wonderful, Nina. I believe I will ask you to send a telegraph to Violet and Drew this week." It would give her maid an opportunity to go see Billy for a little while.

"Oh, miss, that sounds like a good idea." Her maid beamed.

Betsey bade her good night and lowered the lights in the bedroom, getting into bed and pulling up the covers as she settled down.

She didn't go straight to sleep. Instead, she relived the moments when she was whirling about in Vaughn's arms, feeling his hand warm on hers.

Chapter 8

Sunday afternoon started sunny but with a strong breeze. Betsey wrapped a warm shawl about herself as she went downstairs to meet Vaughn. He pulled up to the porch of the hotel in a smart-looking buggy with two horses.

"What good-looking animals, even for work horses," she said.

"They belong to our shop," Vaughn said proudly. "They usually pull a wagon, but I rented the buggy. It's a little cool today, but I don't think it will rain until tomorrow."

He pointed the horses in the direction of Blue Lake. And they were off.

Betsey asked if he'd had a nice time at the dance.

"I should be asking you," he drawled. "It was your first social in Wylder."

"It was so much fun!" Betsey declared. "I loved the cheerful music."

"It is certainly cheerful," Vaughn nodded his head in agreement. "The fiddlers sounded good."

Betsey asked him about some of the people she'd met, and he filled her in on several of the town's leading citizens and others he knew. "Joe knows even more people than me," he admitted. "You should ask him."

"I will," she said.

Once they reached the lake, Vaughn helped her down, and they strolled around the banks of the lake.

"How far do you think the Spaniard Mine is from here?" Betsey asked.

His look was shuttered. "Medicine Bow Mountains are about a two days' ride from here. We'll have to camp out for at least a night or two. We'll be going slower, because we'll have a few pack animals with us."

"Pack animals?"

"Yes, some burrows or work horses to carry equipment."

"That should be exciting," Betsey said. "I've never camped out before."

"What?" He stared at her, his mouth in an *O*. "You're not coming with us."

"I certainly expect to," Betsey said with spirit. "With Nina along, of course. If I'm helping, I want to see the result when you find the mine!"

His mouth set in a hard line. "I don't know about that. It won't be an easy trek. Joe and I didn't expect you would want to go along."

"I may be a city girl, but I am hardy and resilient," Betsey declared.

"Good to know," he shot back. Then his face softened. "I don't mean to sound harsh, but the West is not an easy place to live in. Joe has told me many times it's a far cry from the East coast, 'specially places like New York City. I understand you can get almost anything you want there."

"You make it sound like I'm a spoiled city girl," Betsey said lightly.

"No, you don't seem spoiled." Vaughn studied her.

She felt herself flushing.

A bird called out, breaking the silence. Wind ruffled the nearby shrubs and trees. She and Vaughn continued to walk around the lake, while the horses bent to drink nearby.

The wind was damp. Betsey lifted her face and felt the mist in the air.

She was beginning to recognize the signs of nature here and told Vaughn so. "It's harder to sense nature in New York, with all the smells and smoke, which sometimes obscure the sky and fill the air," she added.

"That must be annoying," he said.

"Yes, but I like recognizing things out here. For instance, I think it's going to rain soon," she observed, feeling dampness once again touching her face.

"You're correct," he said. A moment later, a few drops started to come down. "We better get back before we're all wet."

He led her back to the buggy. The horses had stopped drinking, and Betsey fancied that they were glad to head back to their stable and get out of the rain.

They were soon back in town. By the time they pulled up to the stable and Vaughn and hopped out of the buggy and helped her down, the rain was coming down more steadily.

"Thank you for the ride," Betsey said.

He met her eyes. "I enjoyed it," he said.

She pondered his words. He did look like he was satisfied. She wished it hadn't rained and they could have spent more time strolling around the lake. But she had no desire to get soaked and let Vaughn point her in the direction of the hotel while a lad walked the horses into the stable to unhitch them.

Their walk back was short. Vaughn was silent at first.

"I'm looking forward to our séance Tuesday," Betsey said to fill the void.

Vaughn gave her his skeptical look again.

"Do you really think we'll find the mine using the knowledge we get from the dead?" Disbelief still filled his voice.

She felt a flicker of anger.

"Of course. That's why I'm here."

He inclined his head. "You must be very sure."

"You should be too. You heard the different entities who came through at our séances," she challenged, staring at him. "Including your own brother."

They reached the hotel, and he walked her inside.

"Thank you for a pleasant ride," she said formally.

Taking off his hat, he bowed to her. "My pleasure." He gave her a look she couldn't read and departed, leaving her alone in the lobby.

Humph! Why did this man make her feel such extremes—warm inside one minute, angry the next? Men! She shook her head, wishing Violet was here for her to talk to.

Betsey sighed. She wasn't ready for the afternoon to end, but apparently, Vaughn was.

Maybe she could find someone here to talk to. A glance showed her only an elderly man she didn't know sitting in the lobby, reading a newspaper and puffing on a cigar.

She looked around for Nina, who often frequented the lobby. She'd be grateful to talk to her. She finally spotted her in the restaurant, conversing with one of the waitresses there. At present, there was only one family, finishing a very late lunch in the room.

"Did you want me, Miss Betsey?" asked her maid.

"Our ride ended early because of the rain," she told Nina. "I thought perhaps we could speak more about the dance."

"Of course, miss." Nina always sounded eager to please.

They climbed the stairs together and entered their room.

Betsey gasped.

Chapter 9

"Oh no!' Betsey gasped.

Nina shrieked as they both looked at the disarray in their suite.

Items like books and papers and pencils had been swept onto the floor, as if by an angry hand. Candlesticks rolled on the carpet. Fortunately, they had left the room with no candles burning or a fire could have ensued. Someone had opened drawers in the bureaus, leaving clothes cascading out of them.

This was a matter for the police! And the hotel manager.

Nina was moaning and had her hands to her face. "How terrible! she cried, pointing to the adjoining bedroom. "Look, someone even went through your underthings!" as if that was the worst of it.

"Get the hotel manager," Betsey ordered. "Then please go to the sheriff and ask him to join us, too."

"Should-shouldn't we tell your cousin Joseph?" her maid asked, as she began wringing her hands.

"All right," Betsey replied. "Then get him next." She hoped Nina would be less upset if she had something to do.

Within minutes, the hotel manager was present and said he was unaware of anyone entering the room, which Betsey was sure she had locked. He scurried away to question the hotel's staff.

The sheriff arrived shortly. "Is anything missing?" he asked as he strode about the room.

"I wanted you to see this mess," Betsey said, "But I will check. When my maid returns, we will put it to rights."

Ten minutes later, Nina returned with both Joe and Vaughn. They looked concerned.

Nina and Betsey started straightening up. Nina started with Betsey's undergarments, shoving them in a drawer so they couldn't be seen.

"I'll put these to rights later," she whispered to Betsey.

Betsey wanted to check her notes and the items she used for the séances first.

It appeared nothing was missing, which relieved her greatly. "But someone riffled through my notes," Betsey said. She saw they appeared to be all there, but the pages were out of order. "Thank goodness, they are all here," she told Vaughn and Joseph. She whispered, "I wonder if that was the point of all this. Did someone want information?"

"I dunno," Joe said, and Vaughn added "What information could they get?"

"The location of the treasure, if we had learned it," Betsey stated.

"Perhaps," Joe said.

Nina and she soon had the room put to rights. She hadn't brought many clothes, so it was a simple matter. Nina's things had barely been touched.

The sheriff soon left, promising to try to catch the culprit. Betsey sighed, knowing it was unlikely.

"At least you're safe," Joseph said in a soothing tone,

"Yes," she replied. But was she? She felt very strange about the fact someone had been looking through her things. She shuddered.

Joseph reached out and gave her a hug.

"Thank you for coming," she murmured, directing her glance to include Vaughn.

Both men nodded, but Vaughn's face was set in a grim line. "Be careful," he warned.

After the men left—Vaughn with a backward glance—she sunk into a chair

"Oh, miss!" Nina wailed. She looked near to fainting.

Betsy was glad once again that Nina had excused herself from the séances. She might scare off any spirits!

"Please rest," Betsey urged her. "And when you're ready, go fetch nice lemonades for us both."

"I'll do that first, Miss Betsey. Right away."

Betsey surmised Nina wanted to leave the room for a bit. She reached for her purse and gave Nina the money she needed. Then the young woman scampered from the room, clattering down the stairs.

Well. Betsey surveyed the room, as if she could discern who had been there. Someone had searched the room, perhaps with the intention of stealing information, and with it locked! It made her doubly glad she had brought her maid on this trip. At least, she was not alone at night. She hated the thought of someone sneaking into these rooms.

While she waited for Nina to return, Betsey drew a long, calming breath. Her heart was still beating faster than usual. For now, she needed to relax her tense muscles, so she grabbed one of the books she was reading. She had brought along a romance by a favorite author, along with the books on séances which Drew had given her. She wanted to continue reading the romance.

She was quickly absorbed and startled only when Nina returned. It was obvious the maid wanted to discuss what had happened.

"Do you think they'll be back, miss?" Nina asked as she handed Betsey the lemonade.

Betsey put her book aside and sipped the refreshing drink. "I doubt it. They did not find what they were looking for, so they'll probably give up." Unless they want to try again, she thought.

Nina looked unsure.

"I brought no valuables with me," Betsey continued calmly, thinking of her beautiful ruby and pearl necklace at home.

"I know, miss. I'm thankful for that."

"Yes," Betsey replied. She had been more worried about someone stealing her things on the trip out. Certainly not at a hotel her cousin had chosen!

****

Monday dawned sunny and warm. Tonight they were drawing closer to a full moon. In Betsey's experience, during a full moon, they usually obtained better results from their séances. She hoped the moon would be full on Tuesday.

As she'd promised, she had Nina bring a brief note to the telegraph office, to Violet and Drew. She said that all was fine and she was helping her cousin Joe and Vaughn with some research. She knew they would read between the lines and know she was continuing the séances and all was well.

Nina returned with pink cheeks and a big smile, so Betsey knew she'd had a visit with Billy while she was there.

Betsey tried to have a restful day, sitting and reading during the morning. She told Nina when her maid returned that she would be going for a ride with Haskell Sims and his sister this afternoon.

Nina appeared nervous about staying in the room alone. "Why don't you have your friend join you for tea?" Betsey suggested. "The young woman you were talking to the other day, who works in the restaurant."

"Jeannie? Oh, thank you, miss. That would be good," Nina said with a wide smile. "I'm sure she would enjoy that."

By being there, the two could prevent any break-ins, and Nina would be comfortable, Betsey thought.

Haskell and his sister Louisa were prompt in collecting her. Haskell looked as dashing as usual, and his sister wore a new-looking, smart crimson dress.

As they rode in the rented buggy, which looked like the one she'd been in yesterday with Vaughn, Betsey chit-chatted about life in New York, the parties, and the restaurants. Louisa seemed quite eager to hear about Betsey's life there, asking a whole bunch of questions. Betsey tried to keep up a steady stream of comments in order to avoid answering Haskell's probing questions about their "unorthodox" ways of searching for information on the lost treasure. The less said, the better, she'd decided.

Once they reached the lake, Haskell helped Betsey from the carriage, his hands remaining on Betsey's waist a few seconds too long. She found herself growing annoyed by him taking the liberty and glanced over at Louisa. His sister had alighted by herself.

"Louisa, how do you like living in Wylder?" Betsey asked her, trying to include her in the conversation.

"Oh, it's all right, I suppose," the woman remarked. "But I do miss the excitement of the city of New Orleans."

"And do you want to travel as much as your brother?" Betsey asked as Louisa fell into step with Haskell and Betsey.

Louisa shrugged. "I would be happy to stay in New Orleans. We will probably not stay in Wyoming. I do so miss the city lights."

Betsey turned in surprise to regard Haskell. He was sending his sister a look which appeared decidedly annoyed

"I am here in the West to try to make my fortune," he admitted. "Then I want to visit New York and Europe before returning to New Orleans. Perhaps I will try gambling in London and France." He said it idly, but Betsey was certain that gambling was his motivation for visiting those areas.

"My brother thinks perhaps I will find a suitable husband here in the West and settle down," Louisa said with a pout.

"And do you intend to do that?" Betsey asked, curious.

"No. I think I will be more likely to do so in New York," Louisa said, sending an accusing look at her brother. "I have told him that."

"In New York, you'd be competing with many rich, beautiful women," he said to her.

Louisa glared at Haskell. "I'm not rich—and are

you saying I don't look good enough to attract a man?" she snapped.

"You know I didn't mean that," he said hastily. "I merely meant there are so many women in the city."

She still looked annoyed.

"You are still more likely to find a husband out here," he soothed.

"You always said some of your winnings could be my dowry," Louisa said with another pout. She looked at Betsey. "My parents did not leave us with too much money."

Betsey felt uncomfortable, being in the middle of this spat between brother and sister. She mused that likely, Haskell wanted his sister married so he wouldn't have to support her. Perhaps he even hoped a rich brother-in-law would support *him*. She had met men like him in New York. Gamblers who wanted their families to indulge their wastrel habits.

He turned to Louisa and fired her a nasty look.

Betsey decided to step in. This was obviously an area of contention between the two.

"I have decided to let fate step in and meet my future husband by chance," Betsey said.

"Good idea," Haskell said. "You will meet many men such as myself." He stood up straighter.

"Do your relatives not step in and try to guide your choice?" Louisa questioned.

"My dear mother died recently," Betsey said. "And my elder brothers married women they loved and agree I should do the same if I am so inclined."

A picture of Vaughn flashed through Betsey's mind.

Vaughn? Why did he come to mind when she was

discussing love and marriage?

****

Betsey carefully arranged the candles, drum, and her paper and pencil nearby on Tuesday night. She was ready ten minutes before Joe and Vaughn were due to arrive.

Joe had stopped in briefly after her ride yesterday to see how Betsey was doing. She told him that Nina had been in the room yesterday afternoon with a friend and nothing unusual happened. Although Betsey felt sure that the person had been looking for clues to the Spaniard's mine on Sunday.

"Why else would someone go through my rooms?" Betsey had asked him.

"I agree, the intruder was after some information about the treasure," Joe had declared. "Vaughn suspects that, as well."

Betsey warmed at the thought that they both agreed and cared about her thoughts. Especially Vaughn.

As she waited now, a breeze stirred the curtains. It had cooled a little, and the air was refreshing.

Millie arrived a few minutes early. She asked some questions about what Betsey hoped might occur during the night's séance. Vaughn and Joe followed ten minutes later.

Once they all sat in the dark, with only a few candles to cast some low light in the room, Betsey said, "We are seeking the Spaniard, Carlos Ayala...or his friend, Pedro Martinez...or any other spirits who chose to come through."

The room was silent.

Betsey repeated her request a few minutes later, and the room remained silent for a few minutes. She was about to ask again when she felt a certain heaviness settle near her.

She whispered cautiously, "Who is here? Please introduce yourself."

A voice came from in between herself and Millie. "It is me, Cousin Colleen." The female voice sounded rather young and as if she was struggling to speak.

Millie startled. "Cousin Colleen," she gasped.

"Y-yes." For a moment the spirit stayed silent.

"Oh, please do speak," Millie urged. After a moment, she whispered, "This is my cousin Colleen who died of a fever when she was but eighteen…over two years ago."

"Welcome, Colleen," Betsey greeted the entity. She saw Joe sit up straighter as Vaughn, too, moved in his seat. "Can you help us in our quest?" Betsey asked.

"…not tonight…" the spirit groaned.

Apparently, she was having trouble coming through. There was a brief silence.

"Oh, please do speak again," Millie requested.

"Trying to…" The rest of her words were garbled.

"She is trying," Betsey whispered to Millie.

"Goodbye…"

"I miss you, Colleen," Millie's own voice was shaking. "Please come back."

The spirit whispered, sounding far away.

"My dear cousin…"

The drum slid off the nearby credenza and fell to the floor with a resounding clatter.

There was silence after that. They waited, but the spirit did not speak again.

"Well," Betsey said after several minutes, "I believe that is the end of her visit. Obviously, she had a great deal of trouble coming through."

"But we heard her!" Millie exclaimed. "That was assuredly my cousin Colleen!"

Betsey moved to light the oil lamp. When they sat in the light, Vaughn looked again as if he didn't believe what he'd heard.

Joe bent forward. "Did you recognize her voice, Millie?"

"Yes," Millie said, her own voice tearful. "She sounded as she did when it was near the end of her life…like she struggled to speak and gasped for breath."

"Poor thing," Betsey said. "As she moves farther into the Great Unknown, I believe she will sound more and more like her old self. Tell me, Millie, when did she die?"

"A little over two years ago. We both caught the same illness. But Colleen had more trouble breathing, and so did her younger sister, Marie. Marie was able to survive and is now eighteen. Colleen was very sick and eventually succumbed to the fever."

"Many people in the area of Wyoming fought the same disease," Joe added. "One of our best customers also died, as did the milliner's brother and other people we knew. It was a very sad time."

"I understand," Betsey soothed. "Violet lost a sister the same way, many years ago."

Millie looked hopeful. "But I am so glad to know her spirit lives on!" She sniffled as a tear trickled down her face. She let go of Betsey's and Joe's hands and took out her handkerchief, wiping her eyes and blowing her nose.

Vaughn's expression looked decidedly doubtful.

Betsey turned to him. "You must be feeling more convinced that these visits are genuine," she challenged.

Vaughn shook his head. "No, ma'am," he said slowly.

****

Betsey tried not to let Vaughn's skepticism put a damper on her mood. They were having some minor successes, and she was sure they'd be able to contact the Spaniard or his friend again one of these nights in Wylder. She felt it in her very bones.

Joe believed in their methods, too. And Millie had been impressed by her cousin's visitation. So much so that she begged to help them again before she left.

Betsey hoped that the young woman, excited as she was, would not tell all and sundry that she'd been attending seances.

"Please keep quiet about our séances," Betsey said to Millie before the young woman left with Joe to escort her home.

When they'd all left, Betsey was feeling pretty good about the evening, despite Vaughn's doubtful attitude.

And she still could not fight the attraction she was feeling towards the skeptical carpenter.

Wednesday she took a walk with Nina and Millie and Millie's cousin Marie, who was in town for the day. Marie did not mention the séance so Betsey felt relieved. Millie must be keeping quiet about their séances.

They all went into the general store and looked at fabrics. Then, they visited the milliner, who gave Betsey and Millie the hats they had ordered, and Marie bought one of her own. Betsey offered to buy one for Nina, but Nina said she'd do that another day.

They were still discussing hats when they returned to the hotel. Betsey was again relieved that no one brought up the topic of the séances.

Once they'd returned, she found the clerk had a note for her. Louisa had been by, hoping to go for a stroll with Betsey. Betsey suspected the woman was eager to learn more about New York City, even if her brother wasn't.

Thursday, she awoke to another sun-filled and warm morning. Betsey decided to rent a buggy and ride out to the lake with her paints. Of course, Nina wanted to go with her, "for your safety." She sent a note around to Joe so he'd know where she was and gathered her supplies after breakfast. Vaughn appeared as she and Nina were about to leave the hotel.

"I'm coming with you," he said somewhat brusquely.

"That's not necessary," Betsey protested. "Nina can go with me."

"Yes, it is," he replied firmly. "Joe and I discussed this. Besides the fact that you don't know the area very well, it's not always safe for a woman gadding about."

Gadding about? Betsey fought his idea but was unable to budge him. So she sighed and went along with the plan. She told Nina to remain here. Vaughn might get bored and, therefore, let her go alone next time. Or she would take it up later with her cousin Joe and convince him she was perfectly safe with Nina.

Once they arrived at the lake, she went about setting up her easel and paints. She made it a point to do it by herself, so Vaughn could see she was an independent woman and really didn't need any help.

There was a young girl painting near where she set up her own easel, so when she brought it over she introduced herself.

"I'm Flora," the girl said. "I like to paint and see you do, too."

"Do you live hereabouts?" Betsey asked, readying her brushes. She could see the girl's canvas, and she appeared to be a talented artist. Her painting of the lake with some birds pecking at the ground was coming to life.

"Yes. My father is the undertaker in town, and my mother paints signs and decorates the coffins."

"How interesting," Betsey exclaimed. "I have heard of your mother's talent and seen the colorful signs at the milliner's and other places. Also done by your mother?"

"Yes. There's my brother." The young girl pointed to a boy a little younger than her who was fishing on the lake with another young man who looked to be about the same age as his companion. "And his friend.

They are here to chaperone me," Flora added, wrinkling her nose. "Not that I need anyone."

"I have chaperones, too," Betsey said in a hushed voice. She also made a face. "My cousin Joe's business partner, Vaughn Montgomery, who insisted on accompanying me. Though I'm sure he has other work to do," she said the last loudly, hoping Vaughn would hear.

"You must be Joe's cousin from the East," the girl said. "He has told my mother all about you. She's done some work for Joe and Vaughn—painting some of the decorative wood pieces they've made. And I saw you at the dance Saturday."

"Yes, we were there. It's nice to meet you, Flora."

"You, too." The girl refocused on her painting.

Betsey continued to set up her materials. A glance showed Vaughn lounging in the grass not far away.

She and Flora both painted in silence for twenty minutes or so. A few splashes and exclamations from the boys about catching "big ones" sounded intermittently, but for the most part, it was quiet.

Betsey lost herself in her work. She sketched in the landscape, then began applying her paints. It was as she was doing the tree in the foreground that a cracking noise sounded and something zipped close to her head.

"What is that?" she exclaimed, dropping her brush.

Flora gasped.

At the same time, Vaughn yelled, "Get down!"

Flora dropped to the ground, and Betsey followed suit. Another bullet whipped over their heads, and she heard Vaughn returning fire.

"Watch out!" he yelled to the boys. From the corner of her eye, Betsey saw them sprinting over.

Only moments later, Vaughn neared her, still returning fire.

He dropped down and shielded her body with his own.

Betsey's heart was beating madly from the sudden danger, but now her accelerating heartbeat changed to a different one. She was totally aware of the male body pressed against her back, his warmth, and his protectiveness as he kept her from harm.

Two minutes later, she heard rapid hoofbeats as the culprit sped away.

Vaughn lifted himself awkwardly off her body.

"Betsey, are you alright?" he asked.

She sat up, brushing grass and twigs off her dress. "Yes, I'm fine. Who would shoot at us?"

Flora sat up, as well. "Maybe someone was hunting."

"Then they would have stayed to see if you girls were all right," Vaughn said, his mouth set in a grim line.

Flora's brother and his friend ran up to them. "Who was that?" one of the boys asked.

Betsey had no answer for that, but Vaughn did. "Either someone incredibly careless, or someone who meant one of you harm." He stared at Betsey, his look dark, his eyebrows drawn.

"Well." She shook her head. "I have no idea who that could be."

Vaughn stood up. "Whoever it was, he had to realize he had endangered two women and didn't want to face the music. Are you both sure you're all right?"

"Yes," Betsey replied, and Flora echoed her sentiment.

"I think we should return to town," Vaughn said.

Their peaceful afternoon had been interrupted, and Betsey no longer felt like painting. "All right."

"I agree," Flora's brother said in a take-charge voice. "We should tell Father about this, Flora. Perhaps he can find out who was so—so careless." His words and tone told Betsey he had doubts about the person being "careless."

They began gathering their supplies.

"Do you think someone shot at us deliberately?" Flora asked Betsey.

"I don't know," Betsey said seriously. "But if they

did, to what purpose?"

Flora shook her head. "I have no idea. Are any of us a threat to anyone?"

Chapter 10

It was a good question.

Betsey repeated it to Vaughn on the ride home. "Why would someone try to shoot us? Why are we a threat?"

"Perhaps it's the same person who tried to ransack your room," Vaughn answered, his mouth tight.

That was indeed disturbing. "Then Flora could have been hurt by mistake because of me," Betsey said.

"I don't think the perpetrator meant to harm her," Vaughn said. "But it's true, she was near enough to you to have been hurt."

That was even more disturbing. That a young, innocent girl could have been injured—or worse.

Betsey made a sound of distress. "The sooner we go looking for the mine, the better," she stated.

Vaughn shot her a look she couldn't decipher. She knew she would have to discuss this with Joe. "And we need to practice your shooting again," he said to Betsey.

Vaughn dropped her and her art equipment off at the hotel, then took the buggy and horses back to the livery stable.

As soon as she had left the art supplies in her room, where Nina was reading the romance novel Betsey had finished, Betsey told her what had happened and that she was going to see Joe. Nina gasped and turned white.

"Oh, miss!" She put a hand to her chest. "The West in indeed dangerous!"

"Only sometimes," Betsey argued. "We got back here in safety."

She rushed to see Joe, concerned that Vaughn would give him an exaggerated account of the event because he seemed so worried.

She found him in their cabinetry shop, working on a bench. He paused in his work.

"Vaughn told me what happened," Joe said. "Betsey, I'm very concerned about your safety."

"I'm fine," she told him. She described the meeting with Flora. "Everyone is so worried. Perhaps a hunter aimed carelessly at something."

"You don't really believe that, do you?" Joe asked.

She shook her head.

"No. Someone is trying to thwart our search, I think," she replied. "We must redouble our efforts. Shall we try to contact The Spaniard again Friday night?"

"That's a good idea," Joe said. "Although Vaughn believes it is safer to call off our search."

Betsey's stomach dropped. How disappointing to hear this! "I believe in your dream," she stated, meeting Joe's eyes. "Your dream of finding the treasure. Let us continue, even without Vaughn."

Joe nodded. "I agree."

"And perhaps we should go looking in the mountains straight away," she suggested. "We will be safer than here in town, with so many people."

"Someone must know about our quest," he said, "and hopes to stop it." He set his mouth in a grim line. "I will discuss with Vaughn when we could best go.

We've been trying to get ahead of our orders so we can take a week or two off."

"That is good," Betsey said. "The sooner, the better. Tell Vaughn I shall prepare for a séance Friday night. In the meantime, he's right: Nina and I should have another shooting lesson."

"One of us will take you tomorrow," Joe promised.

****

The following afternoon, Thursday, Betsey and Nina were ready when Vaughn, not Joe, arrived on foot.

"We'll go over to practice at the same place where you practiced before, just outside of town," he said in a determined voice. His mouth was set in a stern line. Betsey imagined that whoever faced Vaughn in a gunfight would face a formidable man.

"Let me show you something," he said when they got to the same location. "You also have to be able to get your gun out quickly in an emergency, when you're facing an enemy." His actions were smooth as he quickly pulled the gun from his holster. "You try it. Imagine taking your gun from your reticule quickly."

He had Betsey, then Nina, try and also practice removing a gun from their pockets. "Many women wear gowns with deep pockets out here for just this reason," he explained.

After a few tries, it got easier. Then he instructed Betsey to do that and aim at the cans.

She tried to do it quickly. But it was more difficult. She only hit one can.

"Practice again," he instructed, after righting the cans.

On her second attempt, she did better. She hit three of the cans.

He had Nina practice next, and she nicked two cans. On her second attempt, she only did two again.

"Now, Betsey, try again," he said.

She was determined to do this better under his tutelage. She tried to quickly pull out the gun and aim carefully.

She hit four cans, knocking over two of them. She squealed. "I'm getting better."

"Yes, you are." Vaughn gave her one of his rare smiles.

Warmth rushed through her, down to her toes. "I want to try again."

He straightened the cans again, then moved in back of her.

She adjusted her stance, pulled the gun out, and shot.

She managed to hit all five cans, knocking over two.

"Very good," he said approvingly. Nina clapped in the background.

"You're next." He nodded at Nina.

Nina took longer to get her gun from her pocket. Then she hit only two targets. On the second attempt, she hit three.

Betsey took a turn next. This time, Vaughn stood behind her.

She was very conscious of him so close. She could feel his breath touch her face. "Keep your feet apart," he said and guided her into the right position.

This time, she hit all five cans, knocking three down.

"Excellent," he praised. Betsey whirled around, finding him closer than she'd expected. Close enough to kiss. But Nina stood nearby, and she knew they couldn't.

Nevertheless, there was a look in Vaughn's eyes that said he wanted to. She warmed at the thought.

And she wanted to kiss him, too. Had they been alone she thought they would have.

But a second later, Nina spoke.

"Well done, Miss Betsey."

And the opportunity was gone in a flash. Vaughn stepped back.

But for just a second, Betsey was sure she had seen that flare of desire in his eyes, that softening of his mouth.

And she'd dream of it tonight.

Chapter 11

It didn't take too long to ready the room for the séance on Friday evening. Then Nina retired to the lobby to read and knit, leaving Betsey alone.

Betsey had relived that almost-kiss with Vaughn dozens of times during the past twenty-four hours. She hoped they would get that opportunity again when they were alone.

Nina continued to be afraid of the séances, now mumbling that it was against her religion, but fortunately, she didn't try to stop Betsey. She was actually more fearful than anything else, Betsey surmised. She had asked about the ones she'd missed, and Betsey always kept her comments brief and unemotional when answering.

Millie had sent round a note that she couldn't join them. Her parents were getting suspicious, and she didn't want them to know about the séances, she said. Betsey was disappointed. She would have enjoyed her company and had wanted her friend to be among the participants. She was sure Joe would miss Millie, too.

The warm day had turned gray and cloudy, threatening rain this evening.

Joe arrived right on time and said Vaughn would be there shortly. He was finishing up some work.

Joe talked about how much he wanted to find the mine. Betsey knew how important the search was to him.

"We must ask for the location again," he said. "Or, for the map his fiend Pedro mentioned."

Vaughn arrived ten minutes later, an annoyed expression on his face. "This may not amount to anything," he grumbled.

As usual, Betsey lowered the lights, and they sat around the table, hands touching. She liked the feel of her hand in Vaughn's rougher one. Joe's was not quite as rough but still comforting.

Betsey asked for any spirits to come through, as she usually did. "We seek answers from the Spaniard," she added. "It is most important to us."

There was silence for a few minutes, and then Betsey repeated her words, asking for the Spaniard's help. "We are trying to find your mine," she said. "If we do, we shall use some of the money to benefit the orphans at the mission and to establish a museum in your name."

Just a minute later, wind gusted through the window, and she felt the familiar heaviness in the air.

"Greetings…" came a rusty-sounding, accented voice. Betsey leaned forward, straining to hear.

"It is I…the Spaniard…Carlos Ayala…" She could hear the voice, and wished it was clearer.

"Welcome," she said quietly. "We are most pleased you are joining us, Carlos. Can you tell us more?"

"The location…of the mine…" She could barely hear him.

"Yes?" Joe asked eagerly.

"The Medicine Bow mountains…northeast corner…" She could hear those words better now. Joe tightened his hold on her in his excitement.

"There is a map…" Carlos rasped out.

"Where?" Joe asked.

There was silence for a moment. "Where is the map?" Joe repeated.

Betsey pressed his hand. If they pressured the spirit, he might resent it. She tried to warn Joe silently with her hand and a look.

"…at Blue lake…" It sounded like the Spaniard was straining to get through.

"On the eastern side…" his continued, as if he was putting in a lot of effort.

"The thickest tree close to the lake…there is a hole…" The Spaniard paused.

Even Vaughn was leaning forward to hear him.

"In the tree…reach in and you'll find the map…" Now, his voice was fading.

"The tree closest to the lake on the eastern side?" Betsey repeated to make sure they got it right. "A very thick tree?" Excitement made her heart beat hard.

At that moment, lightning flashed.

"*Sí, sí…*" The Spaniard's voice faded.

"And we'll find the map there?" Joe asked.

A crack of thunder shook the area and their hotel.

There was silence from Carlos. The only sounds were blowing winds from the impending storm.

"I think he is gone," Betsey whispered. "Although let's wait a few minutes to see."

They waited in the dark room. Just as she was about to give up, Betsey's pen lifted off the credenza and flew through the air, crashing against the opposite wall.

They all jumped in their seats.

And dropped hands.

The candle flickered erratically.

Then the air lightened up, the heaviness gone, and they heard the popping sound that sometimes accompanied the end of a visitation.

"I believe that's the end of our visitation from The Spaniard," Betsey declared. Only the sounds of wind and another low rumble of thunder followed the Spaniard's departure.

"But this is amazing!" Joe stated, standing.

Betsey got up and turned up the oil lamp. "We must write this down." She grabbed her paper and went to retrieve her pen from the opposite side of the room. The pen was cold to the touch.

"This is cold!" she told the men. She shivered. Carlos's ghostly hand had flung it across the room to show he'd been present! She must make a note of that later.

Now, she sat at the table and scribbled his directions first before she took any other notes. She read them aloud.

"At the eastern side of the lake, the thickest tree that is nearest, and it has a hole where we have to reach into. The map should be there."

"Yes!" Joe confirmed.

Vaughn, meanwhile, hadn't said a word, but she surmised that like her, he was repeating the directions in his head.

Vaughn scraped his chair back and stood up. "Well." He cleared his throat. "That's it, then. Let's see if he's correct."

"But we have the information!" Joe's eyes were shining. "We are getting close to finding the mine!" His voice sounded triumphant.

"Yes," Betsey said, a feeling of satisfaction welling up in her. She had helped them with the information they'd been seeking. "Please write your own notes about this evening so we may compare them and see that we've gotten everything down that occurred."

"Okay," Joe said.

"We must keep these notes in a safe place," Vaughn stated firmly. "Otherwise, they could be stolen. The person who ransacked Betsey's room—" he waved a hand—"could return, and we don't know how desperate he may be. Someone has already shot at Betsey."

"Agreed," Joe said. "Since we're almost always at the shop, we should keep them there."

"Good idea," Betsey agreed.

"At least we know what area of the lake has a tree with the clue," Joe continued. He glanced at the window. "I want to get out there." He took a step.

"You'd be crazy to go in this storm." Vaughn put a warning hand on his friend. "At least wait until morning, Joe." As he said the words, rain pounded outside.

Joe reluctantly agreed.

"Can I go with you?" Betsey asked Joe.

"I'll go early," Joe said. "And alone. It will probably look less suspicious to anyone watching our behavior to see me simply taking a ride by myself."

"But that could also be more dangerous," Vaughn said. "I think I should go with you."

"All right." Joe relented. "You're most likely right. It will look like two friends simply going for a nice ride, should anyone be watching our movements."

"Can't I go?" Betsey asked again.

They both turned to her and said in unison, "No."

Disappointment wove through Betsey. But she was also afraid they were right to be cautious. She nodded in acknowledgement, though she didn't like it. "I understand."

The two men left—Joe looking excited, Vaughn more thoughtful. Betsey was certain that Vaughn must believe in the clues they'd received through the séances by now.

What an exciting night! she thought.

****

Vaughn hurried with Joe through the rain and back to the shop. Once there, they shook themselves off and climbed the stairs to their apartment. Vaughn grabbed towels so they could dry themselves completely.

"I'll write the notes immediately," Joe said. "I could put them in the cabinet I made for my bedroom," he continued, "but maybe the shop would be better, I doubt the perpetrator will look in our shop, with all the half-finished cabinets and other furniture. And with us working a lot of hours."

"They're most likely to search in your bedroom, like they did Betsey's room," Vaughn agreed.

"Although it was obvious they also searched her sitting area," Joe added.

"True, but we're in the shop most of the day," Vaughn said.

"I think we should go into the mountains as soon as possible." Joe looked so eager, Vaughn didn't want to sway him. And perhaps he was right.

"We don't have much business at the end of next week, so let's plan to go then," Joe concluded.

"Wait a minute," Vaughn cautioned. "We don't

even have the map yet!"

"We're looking for it first thing in the morning," Joe announced. "Let's study it then and decide on when we're going."

****

Joe and Vaughn were awake early to start their search. They rode out, and as soon as they got to Blue Lake, Joe paced off where he thought the tree should be. "It must be this one," he said, pointing at a thick tree near the lake. He shimmied part way up the tree trunk and, finding a hole, he put his hand inside, feeling around.

"It's empty," he told Vaughn. Disappointment rang in his voice. "Maybe he didn't really put it here."

"Or it's in another tree," Vaughn pointed out, "or someone got to it before us."

"We'll keep trying!" Joe said. "I'm determined to find it."

"Try that one," Vaughn suggested, pointing to a very thick tree at the edge of the woods, right behind the first one Joe had tried.

He held his breath as Joe approached this next tree and scooted up a couple of feet to better reach the hole they could see. Joe thrust his hand inside.

He could see Joe groping around. Then came his triumphant cry, "Got it!"

Joe slid down the few feet to the ground. He clutched a yellowed paper.

Vaughn hurried over to him.

The parchment looked fragile. Vaughn knew Joe wouldn't wait 'til they got back home, and he was right—his partner took a quick look around. Seeing nothing unusual, he spread open the paper. Vaughn peered at it, too.

It was a reasonable sketch showing the Medicine Bow Mountains and pointing the way to a valley over the first foothills. There were written instructions, too.

"Go to the easternmost foothill, up and down the incline, to the second one," Joe read aloud. "Over the second one and into the valley there. Approximately ninety degrees to the right of the biggest boulder, near a tree, there is a cavern. The treasure is hidden there."

"Whoppee!" Joe shouted. He had the widest smile Vaughn had ever seen on his friend's face.

Gladness spread through Vaughn's entire body. Joe wanted this so much! Wanted to be considered good enough for Millie to marry.

And he wanted it, too, Vaughn realized. He wanted the peace of mind and respect that money could buy.

But would it be enough? he wondered now.

Suddenly, Betsey's face came to mind.

He thought of giving up his life as he knew it to spend it with a woman. He wasn't good enough for Betsey, he knew. But did he want to spend his life with someone else? He couldn't picture it. She was the only woman he could imagine spending time with for his entire life.

So what was he to do? Riches by itself would probably mean little to him.

What he wanted, he couldn't have.

Chapter 12

Betsey was up early, excited about finding a map to the treasure. She had been up late the night before, making detailed notes about the séance, then lying in bed too excited to sleep. And thinking back to Vaughn's body pressed against hers as he shielded her from the gunshots the other day and their almost-kiss when she'd practiced shooting yesterday.

She finally fell asleep and dreamed of Vaughn.

When she awoke, she was eager to see him and Joe and learn what they might have found. She knew Joe's intention was to ride out early.

Eagerly she went to eat breakfast with Nina, who was already awake. She didn't linger but rushed through the meal, whispering to Nina only the bare facts of what had happened last night. Then she walked over to Moore and Montgomery Carpenters and Cabinet Makers.

She found them both hard at work. Vaughn hammering something, Joe sanding, and their two employees farther back in the shop, putting together a bookcase.

"We've been expecting you, Betsey." Joe stopped what he was doing and came over to her. In a low voice, he added, "Come upstairs so I can show you something."

Betsey's heart hammered in time with Vaughn's

steady hammering. Joe nodded to his partner, indicating he'd be upstairs. She followed Joe to the apartment. He must have found the map!

Walking into Joe's bedroom, Betsey watched him pull open a bureau drawer. "Here it is." He handed her an old, creased paper.

She unfolded it, her hands shaking. Sure enough, there it was, in cramped handwriting: Directions to the correct cavern in the Medicine Bow Mountains. Beneath the title was a hand-drawn map, showing the mountains and foothills and canyons of a certain area. It was labeled with instructions.

"Go to the easternmost foothill, up and down the incline, to the second one," Joe whispered aloud as Betsey read. He'd obviously memorized the instructions. "Over the second one and into the valley there. Approximately ninety degrees to the right of the biggest boulder, near a tree, there is a cavern. The treasure is hidden there."

Betsey looked up to see Joe smiling triumphantly.

"Yes!" Joe said, pitching his voice even lower. "That's where it is. Vaughn and I had looked deeper into the mountains previously on several trips. It is nearer than we thought. We passed that valley. But now we know where to look!" His voice rose with excitement. Taking the map, he refolded it with the utmost care. "I'm going to hide this in the shop since we will be there all day to watch it."

"How exciting!" Betsey declared. "When are we going?"

"Vaughn and I are going probably at the end of next week. We will have most of our custom orders done by then and can take a break." As if he'd just realized what she said, Joe stared at her. "We?"

"Yes. Didn't Vaughn mention I'm going with you? And bringing Nina, of course."

Joe shook his head. "It's too dangerous, Betsey."

"I insist. I've gotten you this far. It's only fair that you let me see the exciting conclusion."

"No. Vaughn did say something about it, and I told him no. I thought that was the end of it."

"It is not!" She stared at him. "Besides, what makes you think it will be less dangerous if I stay here?"

He hesitated at that. "I'll have to talk to Vaughn," he said reluctantly. "I'm sure Violet and Drew would not approve."

"And I'm sure they would understand," Betsey retorted.

He looked undecided. "I'll speak to Vaughn," he said slowly, reluctantly.

"Do that. In the meantime, we will prepare to go, too." Betsey huffed.

They went downstairs, and Joe slid the paper into a desk drawer that was a floor model. "Vaughn drew a copy that we're keeping in another drawer," he whispered to Betsey.

Vaughn was still bent over a piece of wood he was working on.

An exclamation at the door had them all turning.

Billy, the young man from the telegraph office, rushed in. "There's a telegram for you at the office!" he told Joe. "Old Sid is just getting it now. I'm here to fetch you."

Joe turned to Betsey, his mouth agape.

"The baby," they both exclaimed, and then rushed

to the door. "We'll be back!" Joe shouted at Vaughn.

They practically ran to the telegraph office, Billy at their heels. When they arrived there, Betsey slid to a stop, and Joe nearly crashed into her.

"It's for you, Mr. Joseph," old Sid said, handing Joe the Western Union telegraph paper. Betsey tried to read it, standing beside him.

To Joseph Moore, Wylder, Wyoming."

Violet gave birth to a healthy boy last night. STOP. Mother and baby are doing well. STOP. His name is Charles John. STOP. From your cousin, Drew. STOP.

Betsey let out a shriek. "How wonderful!"

"This is spectacular news!" Joe exclaimed.

He grabbed Betsey's hand, and they danced around the small office.

Billy and Old Sid were grinning ear to ear.

"That's wonderful, indeed, Joseph, Miz Betsey," Old Sid declared.

"We must celebrate tonight!" Joe cried. "Let's go out to dinner at the hotel!"

"Yes!" Betsey agreed. "And let's telegraph them our congratulations," she added.

"Good idea," Joe said. "And, for you," he said, turning to Billy, he put a few coins in his palm.

They rapidly composed their letter.

Congratulations to the entire family. STOP. We are so happy for you. STOP. All is well here. STOP. Love and best wishes. STOP Betsey and Joe. STOP.

Joe walked Betsey back to the hotel after old Sid began sending the telegram.

"He's named for Drew's late brother," Betsey said excitedly. "How perfect. Drew always said he promised Charles' spirit he would name his first son after him."

Joseph nodded, smiling. "Yes, that is wonderful."

Between finding the map, and Violet and Drew's good news, Betsey felt ready to burst with excitement. "I must tell Nina!" she said.

"And I must tell Millie later. About all our good news," he added, his emphasis on the word all. and Betsey knew he wanted to tell Millie about finding the map too

"Just remember to speak softly," Betsey warned him, "when no one else is present." Loudly, she said, "I am so happy for our cousins."

"Yes. As am I." Joe stopped when they got to the hotel. "I'll see you later, Betsey."

"Don't forget to talk to Vaughn," she whispered.

"I won't." And he went on to the shop. As he left her, Betsey noticed the spring in Joe's step.

****

The next few days were filled with plans for the trip into the mountains and starting to pack.

Betsey really wanted to do another séance before they left, but Joe and Vaughn said they were too busy. They wanted to finish up custom orders as much as possible before leaving. Henry and Leon could easily handle the more standard work while they were gone, so they were working late every day.

So Betsey asked Millie if she could come for one last séance before the trip. The following Wednesday night, Millie joined her. Again, Nina declined to come. Betsey had never done a séance with only two people, but she was willing to try.

She'd just finished setting up the parlor section of her suite when Millie arrived.

"I'm so excited that Joe and Vaughn are going into

the mountains this weekend," her friend stated, taking off her hat. "I hope they find the treasure!"

"I hope so, too," Betsey said. "They deserve it."

"You know, the whole town knows you are going."

Betsey and Nina had heard the gossip, too, as they went around the town during the last few days. "I know," Betsey said with a sigh.

"You can't keep a secret in a small town," Millie added.

"So true," Betsey agreed.

They sat down once the oil lamp was lowered.

Clasping hands, Betsey said, "We seek the spirit of the Spaniard and any other entities who wish to come through." And she waited.

After a few minutes of silence, she repeated her request. "We seek The Spaniard and anyone else who wishes to come through."

There was more silence, and she was afraid they were about to be disappointed, with no one visiting them.

But then wind suddenly stirred the curtains, and Betsey felt the familiar heaviness in the air that usually accompanied a visitation.

"Welcome," she said smoothly, her heart beating hard. "Who is visiting us?"

"Colleen." was the prompt response.

Millie stiffened in her chair. "Cousin Colleen!"

"I am here to warn your friends," came the female voice, clearer than the last time she'd visited them.

"Warn us, of what?" Betsey questioned.

"Danger. There is danger ahead," the voice said, starkly.

"From what source?" Betsey asked.

"There are those who mean you harm," Colleen said.

Well, they knew that already. Betsey tried another question.

"Who means us harm?"

"People who want the treasure—for themselves." Colleen's voice became garbled. "Warn you—danger from several—"

"Yes?" Betsey asked.

"Please tell us," Mille pleaded.

"…and Joe…must beware! Must be—on guard—at all times," the spirit gasped out.

Then there was silence, followed by the all too familiar popping noise when a spirit departed.

"I think she has left us," Betsey observed.

"Colleen! Please come back," Millie begged. But there was only the stirring of the curtains and silence in the room.

****

The remainder of the week was spent getting ready for their journey. Joe did try one more time to dissuade her from going, but Betsey was adamant. "I want to help see this thing through," she said. "Besides, if you are unsure which direction you need to take, I can conduct another séance on the way, and we can try to contact either Carlos or Pedro for help again."

"We won't have trouble," Joe assured her.

But Betsey believed she could help and didn't want to hear negative comments.

"It will be rough," Joe said.

"I realize that. But Nina and I are going."

Joe had warned her to pack light, so she and her maid, both kept their belongings to the bare minimum.

Of course, Betsey brought the directions from the séance. Although she was certain they'd all memorized them by now, she didn't want to take any chances.

She tried to let Millie think they were traveling so they could show Betsey "the beautiful scenery" around Wylder. It was better to be cautious and tell people as little as possible, she thought, even though most of the townspeople knew of their journey.. She didn't say a word to her acquaintances. She didn't want the person who'd ransacked the rooms to know, although she did tell the hotel's proprietor, saying they'd be gone a few days. She suspected Millie knew the true purpose of their journey.

Thinking she should throw people off if anyone was asking, she mentioned they might be going to Cheyenne, which she knew was in the opposite direction.

However, she was afraid word got out, as Millie had said. Everyone here seemed to know everyone else's business.

When she told Joe her thoughts he said it was a good idea to say they were headed to Cheyenne, and he had even told his assistants the same thing. "You know how people talk," he said to Betsey. "If the word was to get out that we're searching for the mine again, people might follow us."

"The word is already out, unfortunately," Betsey told him glumly.

Betsey was ready to go bright and early Friday morning. The sun was shining, and the sky was clear. A reluctant Nina accompanied her.

The maid hadn't wanted to go. "It's not proper, us going off with two men," she'd said.

Betsey had sighed. "One of them is my cousin. He'll look after us."

"And it could be dangerous," Nina pointed out.

"You don't have to go." Betsey guessed the maid would dislike her next words. "I'll go myself."

Of course, Nina disliked that idea even more. Betsey's family paid Nina to watch over Betsey, as well as to assist her in all things. So, in the end, she agreed to go with them.

The first hours of their trip were uneventful. Joe said they were taking it at a slow pace, because of the women. "I can handle it if you want to go faster," Betsey said, although she wondered if she really could.

Nevertheless, Joe and Vaughn insisted that they not push themselves, or the horses. Or the two pack mules they'd brought along carrying equipment.

Betsey got to enjoy some beautiful scenery, as they passed through lovely valleys lush with vivid greens, bright flowers, and sparkling lakes. They even passed one small waterfall near a river as they moved west towards the foothills. Betsey vowed to remember the scenery to paint later. When they paused for a lunch break, she took out her pencil and paper and sketched the lake they were sitting near.

Even Nina seemed to enjoy the first day of their journey. After their stop to rest and have lunch, they continued on. The trek was quiet except for the sounds of nature. Once the sun began to lower in the west, Joe signaled they should stop near a quiet lake.

"We've come a good distance, a little more than we hoped, and it's time to rest," he declared.

They set up a temporary camp with a fire. "It will get cool when the sun goes down," Vaughn said. "And you shouldn't overdo it."

"I'm fine," Betsey insisted, though truth be told she was hoping to rest after a day in the saddle.

Her bedroll and Nina's were situated close to the fire for warmth, with the men's bedrolls farther outside the circle of warmth.

"This way, we can hear if anyone or anything approaches," said Joe.

"Even if we don't find the mine, this beautiful scenery has been worth the trip," Betsey commented in an encouraging voice.

They ate the food the hotel's cook had packed for them for their first evening, then, as the sky grew dark, they saw the stars gradually coming out.

The sky looked like lush velvet, and as she watched, little pinpoints of light also glowed through the material. Even the smallest stars winked in the night sky.

Betsey caught her breath. The stars were not so visible in New York City. Even when she stayed at her cousin Drew's home in western New Jersey, which was much more rural than her own townhouse, the sky was not quite as clear as it was here in Wyoming. Here, the stars blazed with vivid light, and you could admire them without obstacles.

She saw Vaughn sitting on the ground on a small rise, staring at the sky. She went to sit near him

"The sky is truly beautiful," Betsey said to him.

"That's the Ursa Major constellation," Vaughn pointed out the bright cluster of stars in the sky. "Captains of ships learn to navigate by the stars. So do many cowboys who are herding cattle and traveling about the West."

"With so many stars, it makes the spot where we are seem like a small part of the universe," Betsey said.

"Someday, men will travel to the stars," Vaughn said. "We won't live long enough to see that; but I know it will happen."

"That sounds so exciting!"

"Yes. It makes me realize there is so much out there that we know nothing about. I'd like to learn about all of it someday." He sighed.

"Like the occult and the afterlife," Betsey said, sighing, too. "I, too, am always reading about those subjects, trying to learn more things."

He turned to regard her full-face. "You are like a scientist, exploring different subjects."

"So are you," she pointed out. "You obviously have learned about astronomy and other subjects. You were not born a good carpenter, either. You learned those skills on your own."

"That is true." Vaugh looked pleased.

Betsey put her hand down on the ground and leaned toward him, wishing she could just impulsively wrap her arms around him. But young ladies didn't do that, she'd been taught. Unless, perhaps, the man was her intended.

He regarded her silently. For a moment, she thought he'd lean forward and kiss her.

"Vaughn." Joe interrupted their reverie. "Have you seen Betsey?"

"I'm right here," Betsey yelled to him, inching away from Vaughn. Their shadowed presence must not have been visible to her cousin, though she felt a pang of disappointment he'd interrupted her time spent alone with Vaughn.

"I got scared, I didn't see you," Joe said, approaching them.

"We were talking about the stars," Vaughn said and stood up. He put a hand down to Betsey. and she took it, letting him help her up.

She wondered if Joe was just being an over-protective male? Surely, he knew Vaughn well enough to know he'd never do anything scandalous.

"Nina says she wants to turn in," Joe said. "It's probably a good idea. The terrain will rise and get rougher as we go farther west, so we need to rest."

"Yes," Vaughn agreed.

"That's fine with me," Betsey said. She led the way back to the campfire.

Once she and Nina had prepared to go to sleep, and slid into their bedrolls, she listened as the men also got ready to sleep. They were discussing the plan for tomorrow's journey and where they would stop and rest along the way.

Her body was tired, and it was a relief to let herself rest in a prone position. The grass was lush enough to make the bedroll comfortable, and she relaxed.

She fervently wished Joe had not interrupted Vaughn and herself at that moment. Would Vaughn have kissed her? Would she have dared to kiss him? She realized it was something she longed for.

Thinking about that exact moment, she drifted off to sleep.

****

Betsey awoke to a beautiful dawn and sounds of the men making breakfast.

She scrambled up, and Nina, nearby, also awoke. She called to the men that they were refreshing

132

themselves and did so behind some bushes not too far away. Apparently, Joe followed them at a discreet distance, so when they walked back to the campfire he wasn't far away.

"We have to be vigilant about watching you two," he told them. "Luckily, both Vaughn and I are light sleepers. If anyone—be it man or animal—approached, we would be instantly awake."

After breakfast, they broke camp and got back on the trail, moving farther west without any incident.

Betsey saw a fox with some kind of prey in its mouth, and Nina remarked on the beauty of the flowers they passed, which had a variety of colors. But over the next few hours, nothing much happened.

They broke for lunch, and Joe announced they were on target to reach the area they wanted to search by late today. "We'll make camp then and begin searching tomorrow morning," he said in an optimistic tone.

About an hour after lunch, Vaughn, who was in the lead, raised his hand suddenly. "Listen." They all stopped. "Do you hear that?"

After a moment, Betsey said, "No."

"What do you hear?" Joe asked.

"I think someone's following us. I'm gonna ride back and check it out," he said.

"Okay," Joe agreed. "I'll lead the way slowly so you can catch up easily."

They moved forward, and about fifteen minutes later, Vaughn rode back, a grim expression on his face. "I didn't find signs of anyone," he said, "but they were probably hiding. I'm certain I heard someone."

Betsey shivered at his grim tone.

"Better to be cautious." Joe nodded his head. "We'll continue on. If you hear them again, let us know."

Vaughn moved to the back of their short line, and Joe once again took the lead.

For a while, they proceeded at a slower pace. Betsey tried to listen carefully, but she didn't hear anything unusual, just the sighing of a slight wind and the calls of birds. Of course, she wasn't sure what she should be listening for.

They continued peacefully on the trail.

One more time, Vaughn said he was riding back to check on a noise he heard, and again when he caught up with them, he reported he didn't find anything unusual.

Still, Betsey had an uneasy feeling after that. She was relieved when they came to the spot where Joe wanted to stop, near a stream.

"We're near our destination. I think we should take turns keeping watch tonight," Vaughn suggested to Joe.

"That's fine. It pays to be cautious," he replied.

"What about Nina and I?" Betsey asked. "We can help." Out of the corner of her eye, she saw Nina shake her head, a frightened expression on her face.

The two men turned as one, and said, "No."

"It's too dangerous," Vaughn said.

Joe added "We know what to listen for."

"We're right where we want to be," Vaughn said in a low voice. "Tomorrow, we can start exploring for the mine."

"This is wonderful," Betsey murmured. 'We can all work together."

Betsey felt it was their turn to pitch in with the cooking, so she and Nina prepared the evening's simple meal of beans, corn, and meat jerky. Joe kept a sharp lookout as Vaughn tended to the horses.

Joe scouted around for a few minutes, after dinner, and announced the area looked safe.

Betsey breathed a sigh of relief. Looking toward the west, she saw the sun was sinking, leaving riotous colors around it.

"I'm going to sit over there," she said, pointing to a slight rise and a large rock perched on top of it. Nina said she wanted to sit by the fire.

Betsey climbed the slight incline and turned to view the western sunset. Farther up here, still close to the campfire where the others were, she spread out her skirts and leaned against the rock. It was good to be sitting on solid ground, and she could relax up here after two long days in the saddle. She could unwind and try not to worry. She spotted Joe watching the campfire, and Vaughn pacing around while Nina stared into the fire. Was Vaughn worried?

She pondered that for a moment, then focused on the beautiful sunset. The oranges mixed with pink and a deepening purple. She hadn't brought her paints with her, of course, since they'd packed only the necessities. But she itched to paint the scene before her.

The snap of a twig behind her had her turning around.

Vaughn had approached almost silently. She hadn't even been aware that he'd moved from their campfire.

"You must always be aware of your surroundings," he scolded, "so someone doesn't sneak up on you."

"You're right, of course," Betsey agreed. "It was just that the colors were so beautiful and vibrant, I lost track of everything else."

He surprised her by chuckling as he plopped down beside her. "Yes, the sunsets in Wyoming and New Mexico are among the most beautiful in the world."

"Tell me," she asked. "Where else have you watched the sun go down?"

"Arizona, California, New Mexico and Mexico, Kansas, and, of course, Nebraska."

"Nebraska?" She watched his face as he answered.

"It's where I'm from." He made a slight grimace, but she caught the expression. There was something about Nebraska he didn't like. He leaned closer. "But these are the most beautiful sunsets."

Her blood was racing at his nearness. "Especially when they're shared," she murmured.

"Yes."

He bent his head towards her, and she tilted hers up. They hadn't had a chance to kiss last night—now—

He brushed his lips against hers. They were soft.

Almost instinctively, her hands went to his shoulders. He brushed his lips against hers again, and this time, her lips clung to his. Their kiss turned fiery in a second, and she was reveling in his strong shoulders, as his lips met hers again and again.

"Betsey," he murmured. She clung to his shoulders; the cloth of his shirt felt smooth beneath her fingers. She could feel the warmth of his body through the light fabric.

The sudden loud voice of Joe interrupted their reverie. Betsey scrambled back as she felt herself flushing all over. And not just from Joe's interruption.

Vaughn had kissed her. She had kissed Vaughn.

And she liked it.

****

The last thing Vaughn wanted was for his business partner and friend to know he was rapidly coming to care for Betsey. He knew she was much too good for him. He'd told himself to stay away. But when she was sitting so close, he couldn't help himself. He wanted to reach out and kiss her, even if it was just this once.

Vaughn stood and helped Betsey to her feet as Joe rounded the tall bushes.

"There you are," Joe said. "For a minute, I was scared, thinking you weren't around." He started to open his mouth to say something else, then shut it abruptly. He sent Vaughn, then Betsey, a speculative look.

Betsey's cheeks grew pink, and she looked prettier than ever.

She said, "We're perfectly safe, enjoying the sunset." Her voice was light.

She moved towards Joe. "We should not leave Nina alone." Vaughn followed her and Joe back to the campfire.

****

Dusk was falling. Soon all the stars would be out, and they'd turn in.

As she got ready for bed, Betsey couldn't help reliving every moment of Vaughn's exciting kiss. She touched her lips. They were still warm where Vaughn had pressed his against them.

She had been kissed by other men. Usually a light peck on the cheek, once a soft brush of the lips by a shy suitor, and one time had a hard and rushed kiss she had angrily rebuffed, by a man who was pressing his suit. That had been the last time she went out with him! But she'd never experienced this tender meeting of lips, which had grown insistent, sending a burning trail of warmth flowing through her insides. A trail of what? she wondered. Was this desire?

She'd heard a few friends and her sister-in-law's titter about the word "desire" behind their hands. Once, Violet had tried describing desire when Betsey asked her how it felt. A yearning, a burning need for *something*, Violet had said. Betsey had wondered as to what that something was.

Now she could guess. A wanting for something just out of reach—plus a desire to be held, hugged. And something more, indefinable. A wanting for this man.

She said goodnight to the others and settled into her bedroll, pulling the material up near her face.

Vaughn. She thought dreamily about him. She admired him. He was hardworking and honest. He was also kind. And handsome.

And she wanted to kiss him!

Could she be falling in love with him? Thinking of him certainly made her feel light and airy, like she was floating. Like nothing she'd ever felt before.

****

Vaughn took the first watch.

Just before they'd made camp, he'd thought he heard someone trailing them again. He'd whispered his thoughts to Joe, not wanting to alarm the women. He'd seen the worry in Nina's face yesterday, although Betsey had looked concerned, too.

Right now, he was too wound up to be tired, although a couple of hours from now, he knew he'd feel differently. So he'd volunteered to do the first watch.

He'd heard Betsey and Nina get settled down, then followed by rumbling snores from Joe.

Then all was quiet.

An owl hooted nearby, startling him, but it was just a natural sound. Was that a whispered word? No, just the wind.

He knew he was being jumpy and possibly scaring the others. But it paid to be cautious. He was positive he had heard a horse behind their party several hours ago. Though he'd found no evidence of anyone following them, it didn't mean no one was shadowing their group. He was certain he'd heard it, and he rarely mistook these things. The feeling of being followed was something he couldn't shake. His Indian heritage had kicked in, his instincts warning him.

He looked over at the others, lying so peacefully. Once in a while, Betsey moved a tad, and she murmured something unintelligible.

Betsey. Had there ever been such a sweet, innocent, and pretty young woman in Wylder? He couldn't think of any. The only women who'd caught his eye in the last ten years had been the tarts you always found hanging around where there were men with money. And they'd been temporary diversions. No. No one else had made him look twice. Certainly no other innocent young lady, like Betsey Chalmers.

She was so beautiful. He itched to run his fingers through the silky strands of her golden hair.

And she had a positive outlook, a sparkling personality. As if she thought the world was wonderful.

She hadn't been disillusioned by life yet.

He knew he had been.

But a relationship with Betsey was not to be, he knew. Vaughn Montgomery wasn't worthy of a sweet young thing like Betsey. He was a half-breed, though he recalled that fact less and less often. Out in Wylder, people didn't seem to care as much as the folks east of here. He liked the fact that many of the people he'd met in Wylder judged a man for himself, not for his heritage. He'd met people who were Scottish, Irish, German, and Chinese. But there were still people around who would remind him of his race and taunt him, even in this friendly town.

And he couldn't dare hope to gain Betsey's love. Wyoming might be a place where a man could be judged for himself most of the time, but still, he wasn't the man for Betsey. He knew it. Perhaps she didn't, or she regarded him as a challenge. Their almost-kiss had had him momentarily dreaming about winning her regard. But that was not to be.

With a sad sigh, he sat back and listened to the night sounds.

Chapter 13

Dawn was just breaking when Vaughn awoke.

He glanced over to see Joe was already at the campfire, making coffee.

When he reached his friend, he said, "I guess you're eager to get started."

"You bet I am." Joe sat back, waiting for the coffee beans to brew in the heat from the campfire.

"Should we wake the women?"

Joe glanced over to where Betsey and Nina were still sleeping peacefully. "Nah. Let's let them rest for a few minutes."

Joe gritted his teeth. Vaughn could see his friend was chomping at the bit, eager to get started on their quest for the cave that held the treasure.

But Joe surprised him. "How do you feel about Betsey?"

"What do you mean?"

"You know what I mean, Vaughn. I mean how do you really feel about her? Emotionally? In a romantic way?"

Vaughn felt a pang in his middle. "It doesn't matter how I feel, Joe. She's too good for the likes of me."

"Don't say that! You told me I was good enough for Millie's family when they didn't accept me. The same applies to you."

"But you're not a half-breed," Vaughn said. "I've

seen how people react to that."

Joe pursed his mouth. "Not out here in Wylder. This town is more accepting than most. Besides you're a well-respected businessman, hard-working, and commendable. And from what I've learned from my sister, Betsey's family is not prejudiced. Why don't you give this thing with Betsey a chance? You know as her only relative out here, I totally accept you." He waved his arm, including the two sleeping women in his dramatic sweep.

Vaughn sat back. Could there be any chance for him and Betsey? he wondered.

****

She smelled the robust aroma of coffee.

Betsey opened her eyes to see that dawn was here. This could be the day they found the treasure.

She scrambled out of her sleeping bag. Nina was starting to stir. The two men were sitting around the campfire.

"I'm going to take care of business," she hissed to them, then found the large clump of bushes.

Returning to them a few minutes later, she saw Nina was now sitting up. She took a mug and Joe said "good morning," as he poured her a cup of coffee.

"Good morning. It's a fine-looking one! We might find the treasure today!" she said.

Joe gave her a big grin. "That we might."

They were soon having a quick breakfast. In the interest of efficiency, they broke up into pairs. Agreeing it was unwise to work alone, working in pairs with one man, one woman was the safest, Vaughn had said. Both Joe and Vaughn were excellent shots, if there were any dangerous occurrences. Plus, they both knew what signs of gold to look for.

Once they found the treasure, they would bring rock samples back with them to Wylder and claim the mine. They could then hire more men for a larger expedition, and then return with a good amount of gold and prepare for a large mining operation.

"That's if we find it," Vaughn cautioned.

She was disappointed that Vaughn was paired off with Nina, leaving her with Joe. Had Joe wanted it that way after witnessing them together the other day? Or did Vaughn not trust himself around Betsey?

No one found any success in the first hour of searching.

Once, Betsey thought she saw the gleam of metal. But it turned out to be a bullet shining through dirt.

"That's not it," Joe said, sounding discouraged. Then he turned to Betsey. "How are you feeling about Vaughn?"

"Feeling?" Betsey questioned. Joe must have realized that she and Vaughn had almost kissed the other night. And perhaps he saw the kiss they *did* share yesterday. "I like Vaughn. A lot."

"Yes, but do you love him?" he asked directly.

Betsey slowly straightened. "Do I love him? Honestly, I don't know." She'd been afraid to consider it, afraid of her feelings. And frustrated because she'd been unable to really share her emotions with another woman she was really, really close to. "Maybe. I don't really know. I'm not sure what love is."

"I can tell you." Joe's expression was serious. "You think about the other person all the time. You want to be near them. You want to be close, physically. You care about what happens to them and their feelings. And you feel a desire for them."

As he said the words, Betsey considered them. Yes, she thought about Vaughn constantly. Yes, she wanted to be near him. She wanted to be close. She cared about what he thought and felt. And she liked kissing him. She wanted more. And she thought she was experiencing desire for the first time in her life.

She stared at her almost-cousin. "Yes, I think I do."

****

Betsey had more time to ponder her own revelation that afternoon.

"We've been following the directions the Spaniard's map gave us," Joe declared, his voice tinged with disappointment.

"I know," Vaughn said. "Maybe he was wrong."

Betsey hated to see the man she cared so much for, and her cousin, getting discouraged.

"We just started the search," she said. "We're not going to give up."

Joe sent her a grateful look. "That's right."

They discussed moving to the next valley, and they moved there after lunch.

She noticed Vaughn kept looking around behind them.

"Do you think someone is following us?" she asked,

"I have not heard anything with my ears," Vaughn replied. "But my instincts say yes." He looked at Joe. "Give me a few minutes when we are on top of the rise to scout around."

"Go ahead," Joe said.

Nina sent Betsey a look. Betsey knew her maid was getting scared.

"It's all right," she told Nina. "I don't think we're in danger." But inside she was not so sure.

****

They moved to the next valley without incident. Vaughn came back from his scouting to report he hadn't seen anything unusual.

"We've been following the directions from the map the Spaniard 'gave' us," Joe repeated. "I don't want to think he was wrong."

Betsey sent him an encouraging look. "We're on the right track. I'm sure of it," she told Joe cheerfully.

"You're right. We must not give up." He pointed. "I think there's a cave there, behind those bushes."

They entered the cave. It was shallow, but they checked it thoroughly without luck.

Vaughn and Nina were checking the other side of the valley.

They all continued to search, until late in the afternoon as the sun began to dip slightly in the sky. Betsey could see Joe was beginning to look discouraged again.

"Let's break for the day," she suggested, when they came out of the third cave they'd found. "And start fresh in the morning. We can move to the other side of the rise where Vaughn and Nina are, if they're done, too."

"We have one more patch of land on this side," Joe said stubbornly. "If you're tired, I'll check it alone."

"I'll go with you," Betsey said. "Safety in numbers, right?" She tried to make her voice cheery.

They explored the last area on this side of the foothill. There were no more hidden or obvious caves. Joe looked dusty and weary when they finished, and she was sure she did, too.

"All right," he said slowly. "Let's meet up with Vaughn and Nina."

They found the pair, who were finishing up their side of the valley. They all agreed they were tired and hungry. They went back to where they'd left the horses and mules in the center of the valley under shady trees, and set up camp.

"I know—let's have a séance and contact the Spaniard again!" Joe suggested.

"Good idea!" Betsey said. "We can ask him for more specifics."

Vaughn shook his head. "I don't think we'll be able to. We've had trouble contacting him before."

"But why not try?" Betsey asked. "It won't hurt to do so."

****

They sat around the campfire once it grew dark, holding hands. The night was punctuated by the crackling of the fire. Vaughn held her hand loosely. It was almost like he was reluctant to touch her, she thought.

Betsey had prevailed on Nina to join them. The men were concerned about anyone being too far away, and she knew they were right, there was much more safety if they all stayed together. Their guns were within reach.

"We call upon the spirit of Carlos Ayala," she began in a soft voice. "Also known as The Spaniard in these parts."

There was silence. A slight breeze rustled the tree leaves.

After a few minutes, she tried again. "We are

seeking the spirit of Carlos Ayala."

There was another breeze sweeping through the night air, and then she felt that heaviness in the air that sometimes happened when a spirit joined them.

"It is I, Red Feather," the deep voice intoned.

Nina started.

"Thank you and welcome, Red Feather. Can you help us contact The Spaniard, Carlos Ayala?" Betsey asked.

There was a pause, and then, "I am here, amigos." In the familiar, but rather hoarse, voice of The Spaniard. Betsey thought perhaps he had smoked tobacco often during his life. His voice had the coarse and harsh quality of a smoker.

Behind them, the fire flared momentarily.

"Carlos, we have tried to find your mine without success. Can you help us?" Betsey held her breath as they waited for an answer,

"*Sí, sí*...there was a cave-in at the original entrance."

She heard Joe suck in a loud breath.

"But," Carlos continued, "There is another entrance and exit farther along the cave. If you go to the next valley, you will find it—easily enough after the—first slope. All the way on the right." He sounded like he was gasping for breath.

He must be having difficulties coming through, Betsey surmised. She let out her breath in a whoosh.

"Many thanks," Joe declared.

"Yes," Betsey added. and Vaughn and Nina nodded their heads. Betsey could see Nina's eyes were wide, and Vaughn's mouth had softened from its grim line. Joe looked happy, a smile lighting up his face.

"We will look on the morrow," Joe added.

"Thank you so much," Betsey added sincerely.

"Yes, thank you," Nina whispered.

"Thanks, Carlos," Vaughn said.

"I cannot stay. Once you find the mine, I will be leaving for the Great Beyond…" His voice was starting to fade.

"We understand," Betsey said.

"We will build a museum and give money to the orphans at the mission," Joe pledged.

Then there was no more talk, just that peculiar popping noise.

****

The following morning, as they sat around the campfire eating breakfast, Joe suggested they search together since he was pretty sure they'd find the right cave after contacting Carlos Ayala.

"That's a good idea," Vaughn echoed.

So, they quickly finished eating and went on their quest.

"Look!" Joe exclaimed, pointing to an opening on the side of the foothill. He lost no time rushing there, with Betsey, Vaughn, and Nina on his heels.

Joe stepped inside the opening. It was about six feet high and narrow at the opening, but it widened considerably a few feet in. Vaughn lit a lantern and held it high.

There were shining gleams here. Joe and Vaughn dug around. Betsey found herself holding her breath.

"Looks like it!" Joe exclaimed suddenly. "We got it!"

"Looks like it," Vaughn agreed, sounding cautiously optimistic.

They dug around some more. And Joe held up a stone. "Here it is!!" he exclaimed triumphantly. "Gold!"

They gathered around him.

"Sure looks like it," Vaughn said. He grinned as widely as Joe.

"Let's get the equipment," Joe exclaimed.

They decided Vaughn would stay here temporarily and keep watch while Joe, Betsey, and Nina moved the horses and mules closer to the cave, with the minimum of equipment they'd brought along.

They soon had the animals down in the valley below and were back together. Joe and Vaughn started digging in the spot where Joe had found the piece of gold, while Betsey and Nina scouted the cave for any other signs that looked promising.

"Don't go too far back," Vaughn cautioned them.

They worked for several minutes. "Here," Betsey said, spotting the gleam of gold some yards from the men. She instructed Nina to put a stick there so they could easily find it again later.

****

They were digging enthusiastically when Vaughn heard a noise outside. "What's that?" Vaughn drew his gun almost by instinct.

One of the horses snorted, and another one moved restlessly.

"They heard something," Joe whispered.

Vaughn slowly inched forward, out of the cave, and looked at the four horses and the pack mules, where they stood in the shade, protected from the hot sun. They were also out of sight from prying eyes.

Nina started to speak. and he whispered, "Hush!"

Vaughn strained to hear. Was that a footfall, perhaps? Betsey thought. They all listened.

And into the silence, they heard small rocks skitter, as if underneath a heavy foot.

Vaughn crept farther forward and peered about. He stepped farther away a few seconds later.

"Halt!" he yelled and disappeared down the side of the foothill.

Joe ran after Vaughn.

****

Nina looked at Betsey. "What could be out there?" The maid's voice trembled.

"Perhaps another rider," Betsey conjectured. But who could it be, this close to the cave's entrance? Was Vaughn right, and someone was truly following them?

'Let's see what's going on," Betsey suggested. She led the way to the front of the cave.

Nina cautiously made her way behind Betsey.

Betsey peered out. At first, she just saw swaying trees. The wind had picked up. Then she heard steps.

She pulled back, Nina cowering behind her.

"It's Joe," Betsey announced, spotting her cousin.

Joe entered the cave with Vaughn a few steps behind him.

"There *was* someone there," Vaughn said, his mouth grim. "But when I went after him, he ran away and then took off on his horse."

"Did you see what he looked like?" Betsey asked.

"Medium-sized fellow. He had a hat pulled low so I never saw his face," Vaughn said. "But he must have been following us, skulking about."

"Why do you think he was?" asked Betsey.

"Either he's snooping, and our party had him

curious," Vaughn stated, "or—and this is more likely—he knows about our search and has been following us for several days."

"I don't like it." This came from Joe.

"Neither do I." Vaughn words were harsh.

****

They continued their search. As he worked side by side with Joe, searching for more evidence of gold, Vaughn felt hope rising in his chest. He'd told himself not to hope much. He'd told himself it was a long shot. Still, apparently his dreams were pinned on the idea that they would find the treasure they sought and become more than comfortable, not simply by their hard work, but because of a chance they would find the Spaniard's lost mine. They could be rich!

He knew Joe was pinning his hopes on the fact that he would become wealthy, and he would be allowed to court Millie. There must have been some of that in him, too. Because he had dared to consciously think that someday he would curry favor with Betsey.

But money, he reminded himself, would not take away the stain of his mixed heritage. He was proud of being half-Indian. But the world did not see it that way. People thought less of him because of his mixed blood.

Even if Betsey seemed unaware—or unconcerned—about his humble origins, others would judge them. And money would not change that fact.

True, in this community of Wylder, men were known not for their ancestry, but for their hard work that led to success. And he was proud of that fact also.

Still, his blood would be considered by some as impure. And he wouldn't want to pass on that background to any potential children. He'd have to settle for a poorer woman, not one who came from an upper-class family. But he couldn't picture it. Whenever he thought of settling down, Betsey's face came to mind.

"When is the best time to lay claim to this mine?" Joe interrupted his confusing thoughts.

"The sooner, the better," Vaughn answered, wiping his brow.

"Agreed. Why don't we pack up tomorrow morning and head back to Wylder then?" Joe suggested.

"Sounds like a plan," Vaughn agreed.

They found what looked like a rich vein of ore just before midday and showed the pieces to Betsey and Nina. They paused to eat lunch near the horses.

"Is it as rich a find as you hoped?" Betsey asked.

"The pieces we've found so far are," Joe asserted. He added, "we'll be back in Wylder in a few days. We'll stake our claim for this mine immediately and pack up so we can start our return journey. Once we've been to the land office, we can head back here with more men, including some we will pay to be guards, and you women can stay in town."

Nina gave a loud sigh of relief.

Betsey sent her cousin a look Vaughn couldn't read. Was she eager to get back to Wylder, or not?

They continued searching after lunch, digging at the rocks, with small pickaxes. Vaughn grew warm as the sun heated the air, even in the damp cave.

"Here's another rich vein," Joe declared, "to the left."

Vaughn went to see what he'd found. "Looks like it. Great work."

At that point, the women excused themselves to find bushes to relieve themselves, as the men had done an hour earlier. After they left, he felt the hairs at the back of his neck stir.

Were they in danger? Should he have gone with them?

He turned but saw nothing unusual as he scanned the area by the cave.

He turned back to Joe, who was working diligently. He joined his friend again.

They worked for a few minutes, and then Vaughn heard a noise behind him. His instincts kicked in.

Someone was there!

"Nice find, fellows. Too bad I'm the one who'll enjoy it. Hands up," came the order from the mouth of the cave.

Ice filled his lungs as Vaughn slowly turned. He started for his gun.

"Not so fast." The voice came from the gambler, Haskell Sims. He stepped into the cave.

Joe made a sound of distress, then raised his hands.

"You, too, half-breed," Haskell ordered. "And don't go for your guns or I'll shoot."

Chapter 14

Betsey knew the men were eager to formally lay claim to the treasure. But she was not so eager to get back to town.

For one thing, once they did, she'd be without Vaughn's company for a week or two. Or more. Secondly, they would no longer need her. She had achieved what they wished for the most: finding The Spaniard's Mine. They'd been successful in their quest, because of her guided seances.

There was no longer a pressing need for her to stay in Wylder. Indeed, she knew Nina was hoping to go back East as soon as they could. The men no longer required her presence.

Betsey did not feel the same as Nina. These last few weeks had been wonderful. Time spent in a town she really liked, doing something to help both business partners. Time spent with the man she was rapidly coming to love.

"Besides, I want to see the men become rich and successful from this find," she mumbled to herself. She finished her business and went several yards to where Nina was. "I want to see what happens with Joe and Millie," she said so that Nina could hear. And to see where she and Vaughn could be headed, she said silently. Could they ever achieve a serious relationship?

Then she and Nina started walking back to the

cave.

"I hope so much that Cousin Joe will be rich and successful after this find," she said in a low voice to Nina.

Nina looked at her sideways. "And Vaughn, too, miss?"

Betsey blushed. "And Vaughn, too," she replied softly.

They drew closer to the cave.

That was when she heard the man's menacing voice. "Kick your guns over here."

When she drew closer, she could see his back as he faced into the cave, probably squaring off with Joe and Vaughn. The man appeared to have his gun drawn.

He was threatening them!

****

Betsey drew a sharp breath.

Behind her, Nina gasped.

Betsey turned slightly and put her finger to her lips, warning Nina to be silent.

She could hear the sounds of guns being thrown down, the skitter of one across the dirt floor of the cave.

"That's right," the man warned. "Don't you try anything funny."

Haskell! She recognized his voice.

Was he alone?

Betsey turned and rapidly scanned the landscape. It appeared Haskell had no accomplices nearby.

She took a silent step closer, than another. She reached for her gun.

When she'd removed it from her pocket, she trained it on Haskell's back.

"Don't you try anything funny, either," she loudly

warned Haskell. "Turn around and drop your gun."

He startled, straightening, and turned around slowly. Glaring down at her, he said, "You won't use that, Betsey darlin'."

"I certainly will," she declared coldly, stiffening her spine. "Drop your gun."

He hesitated.

"Drop it!" she ordered.

He took a step closer, and without another thought she shot at the ground near his foot.

That stopped him. "Aw, Betsey," he whined, "I was hoping we'd share in this treasure. Once we get back to Wylder, I'll buy you anything you like—pretty dresses and jewels. Just give me the chance to set you up and marry you like you deserve—"

"Stop talking," she said, anger boiling inside her as he refused to drop his gun. He wanted to kill Vaughn and Joe! And she had no doubt he'd kill her and Nina, too. "I'm not a fool. Drop your gun now."

He slid over another step towards her, still holding his weapon.

Betsey raised her gun, aimed, and fired.

Chapter 15

Haskell collapsed.

Vaughn sprinted over to him and took the gun from his hand. Only then did Vaughn look him over carefully, rolling him over and feeling by his heart.

"He's dead."

Joe ran over to Betsey and hugged her, slipping her gun from her shaking hand.

"It's all right, cousin," he said affectionately, hugging her to him.

"I didn't mean to kill him," Betsey cried as she stared at Haskell's still body. Joe offered her a handkerchief. "I only wanted to hurt him enough so he—he wouldn't be a threat to everyone!"

"It's all right, you did the right thing," Joe soothed, hugging her closer as she trembled in the aftermath. "Betsey, he would have killed me and Vaughn, then he would have killed you and Nina."

"Oh, miss!' Nina launched herself at Betsey, hugging her, too.

Betsey slumped against Joe, her body shaking in the aftermath. "I...was afraid...he was going to...kill us."

"I know, I know," Joe said. "And he would have."

"Miss Betsey, you did good." Nina sniffled into her own handkerchief.

"I know," Betsey said, "but I only wanted to

wound him—so we could bring him back to Wylder, to the sheriff—"

"It's better this way," Vaughn cut in, "and you gave him fair warning, He would have killed us all, Betsey. Nina's right—you did good. In fact, he died instantly, so it was a swift and merciful death. Better than a hanging."

He came over to where she stood with Joe and Nina and wrapped his arms around them all. "Justice was served."

"Do you—do you think so?' she asked, ending with a hiccup.

"I truly do."

"So do I," Nina said.

"As do I," Joe finished.

Betsey tried to stop her tears. She'd killed a man. A very bad, evil man. It had been to save the others, especially the man she loved. But…she'd killed Haskell Sims.

Joe pulled back and smiled down at her. "I'm proud of you, Betsey. You aimed true and killed our enemy."

"I didn't mean to," she sobbed, the tears starting again. "I thought I would wound him."

"Come, sit down," Vaughn urged, pulling her arm from Joe and leading her to a large, smooth stone near the cave's entrance. Once she was sitting on the slab, Betsey put out a hand against the cold stone to steady herself.

"Nina, can you get her water?" he asked.

Nina scampered to get one of the canteens near the cave's entrance and offered it to Betsey. She drank a few gulps of the cool water, letting it slide down her dry throat.

"Thanks," she whispered.

"I think she needs more than water," Joe advised. "I have a small flask among my things—"

"No, I'm—all right," Betsey said.

"We need to make sure Sims had no accomplices," Vaughn said in a gruff voice.

"I looked around before I threatened him," Betsey told them.

"I'll check again. You all stay here." Joe hurried away. Moments later, she could see him riding his horse.

"Have more water," Nina urged, and Betsey complied.

****

She'd shot a man dead. She was spectacular.

Vaughn studied Betsey as she sat on the rock, still trembling but breathing slower. He'd never admired a woman more.

She'd killed their enemy, a man who he'd had no doubt would have killed them all without compunction.

He'd never liked this gambler. He was too slick, too uppity. But he hadn't known Sims was the one who meant them harm.

Sims must have been following them for days. Vaughn's instincts had told him they were being shadowed, but he didn't know by whom. Although he could guess it was because someone wanted to share in their discovery and claim it as his own. Someone too lazy to do his own research and find his own mine.

"Thanks," Betsey said shakily to Nina who had placed an arm around her.

"Are you all right?" he asked Betsey anxiously.

"That man would've killed us all, I have no doubt."

Betsey pushed some hair behind her ear." "I know that. I meant to injure him and stop him," she repeated. "I never meant to kill him."

"This is better," he insisted. "We would've had trouble getting him to the sheriff, and if he was working with others, they could have tried to sneak up on us."

"I believe it," Betsey said. "It's just,...a hard thing to accept. Killing a man."

"He meant to hurt us all," Nina said.

Betsey nodded. She believed that.

Nina moved to sit on the grass beside the rock, and Vaughn lowered himself to sit right beside Betsey on the rock, taking her smooth hand, which was cold despite the warm temperature.

"It's all right," he said in a soothing voice to her. "You're very brave, Betsey. You did what you absolutely had to."

She nodded.

They were quiet, and as he held her soft hand he wished he could do this again and again. Protect her, reassure her. Treasure her.

Spend his life with her.

He started at this sudden thought that had pierced his brain. Spend his life with Betsey Chalmers? Once the thought took root, it held on there. He loved Betsey. He wanted to spend his life with her.

But was afraid it was impossible. She was too good for him.

His gut clenched with a pang of longing. He stared at Betsey, wishing things could be different.

They heard the *clip-clop* of horses, and he knew it was more than one.

Standing, he drew his gun, pointing it at the top of the hill, where horses were rapidly approaching from the other side.

"Shh," he said to the women. "Take cover." He inclined his head towards the cave.

Betsey and Nina scrambled up and dashed to the cave, where he knew they would watch. He trained his gun on the top of the hill.

"I'm back," Joe yelled.

Vaughn let his body relax, but only somewhat. He still kept his gun on the top of the hill. What if someone had captured his friend and was forcing him to say that?

The horses approached from the other side, drawing nearer. They would appear at any minute.

He heard Betsey take out her gun. Then the sound of Nina doing likewise.

A woman on horseback crested the hill.

Haskell's sister! He recognized her at once.

Joe appeared behind her seconds later. His own gun was trained on her back.

Vaughn heard Betsey's sharp intake of breath.

"I found Louisa skulking around, waiting for Haskell," Joe called.

It was perfectly clear that Joe had captured the woman, following her with his gun aimed at her in case she tried to escape. Her body slumped on her horse, her head bowed in submission. They came to the bottom of the valley where they stopped, and Joe slid off his horse, still watching her carefully.

"You can get off now. I'm going to tie your hands together," Joe said, and she complied.

Vaughn could hear now that she was crying, and as soon as she was off her horse, her cries became bawls.

"He made me do it," she sobbed. "I didn't want to come on this trip, too. And I-I can't believe Haskell is dead!" Now the woman turned to glare at Betsey. "Why did you have to kill him?"

"I'm sorry," Betsey said. "I wanted to injure him. He was threatening us and needed to be stopped."

"He wasn't going to kill anybody!" Louisa cried. "He just wanted the treasure. Then we wanted to go to New York, spend a little money. He didn't want to hurt anyone!" she shrilled.

"He would have killed us all," Vaughn stated. "He only wanted the gold." He kept his gun on her. "I'll take over, Joe. Good work on capturing her!"

Joe smiled as Vaughn went to stand by the woman, who dropped to the grass, sobbing.

"He would never hurt anyone, not really!" she insisted. "He just wanted the treasure, and Haskell was a good man. He'd just made the mistake of gambling away the last of our money! He would have gotten his share of the gold and taken care of me, as I deserve to be taken care of! He promised!" She cried harder.

Vaughn and the others stared at her. Was she so naïve? he thought. Or was this simply a ploy to get them to let her go?

****

They made camp early that evening, on the other side of the valley, where they'd camped last night, after they put a stake right outside the cave, carving their names in the wood.

. Betsey knew Joe thought it would be better for her to be away from a view of the cave. He and Vaughn had buried Haskell near the top of the hill, as Louisa had requested, so "he'd be nearer the Heavens," as she put it. They all stood around the grave for a moment of silence, and Joe asked for peace for his soul and forgiveness. Afterwards, they'd prepared supper, except for Louisa, who had her hands tied until they sat down to eat. Then she was allowed to eat with them, with Vaughn and Joe carefully watching her like the hawks that had circled near her brother before the burial.

Joe poured a generous tin cup full of whiskey for Betsey. "It will help settle you," he advised.

She thought she would have trouble sleeping, but between fatigue and the whiskey, she easily drifted off to sleep while the men were murmuring by the fire, making their plans.

The following morning, they were up at dawn, eating a quick breakfast, and breaking camp. They took turns watching Louisa, even Betsey and Nina watching her as they held guns. No one trusted the woman.

Once they were on their horses, Joe led their expedition, with Betsey following, then Nina, then Louisa, with Vaughn bringing up the rear and keeping an eye on Haskell's sister. Joe also led the pack mules and Haskell's horse. They wouldn't abandon the animal, and it could be sold and the money given to Louisa, who had none right now. She might want a lawyer since she'd be facing charges.

At this point, Betsey doubted Haskell's sister was a threat. The woman slumped in her saddle, sometimes sniffling or crying.

Their trip down the foothills was uneventful. They took a break for lunch, then continued. The weather was fair, and going down the slopes took less time than going up, even with the extra person in their party. Joe and Vaughn had switched places after lunch, and

Vaughn was now leading. They must have made excellent time since he declared they would make camp near a small river, earlier than she expected.

After dinner, Joe suggested she take a walk with him. They left Nina and Vaughn to watch Louisa by the campfire.

It was good to walk around after being in the saddle all day.

"Are you all right, Betsey?" he asked as they strode away.

"You mean—because of shooting Haskell? Yes, I think so," she answered honestly. "I did feel bad, until I thought about how he was threatening you and Vaughn."

"Yes." Joe nodded. "You did good, Betsey. Really, really good. You were brave and did what you had to in order to save us *all*." He looked at her, smiling.

They walked in silence for another minute, until they were out of sight of the fire. Then he turned to face her. "And how do you feel about Vaughn?"

She stared at Joe. "I-I care about him. A lot," she admitted.

"Care? As in you love him?"

Betsey swallowed. "I-yes. I do." Satisfaction wove through her. Saying the words made her feelings more clear, more firm.

"Ahh. I thought so," Joe said, with a pleased smile. "It's fine, Betsey. I won't tell him what you said."

"But I'm afraid—" she went on.

"Of what?"

"That he doesn't feel the same."

"Oh, I think he does." Joe took her hand and squeezed it.

164

But Betsey shook her head. "He hasn't said anything to me."

Joe turned and started leading her farther away. "That's because he's afraid."

"Afraid?" She let Joe lead her, taking careful steps as they walked a small trail that followed the river.

"He thinks most women wouldn't want, as he put it, a half-breed," Joe said.

Betsey stared at her cousin. Vaughn—a half-breed? But as she recalled his sympathies for any Indians they'd met, and his dark good looks, it made perfect sense that he was half-Indian. And she remembered Haskell had called him a half-breed. She'd meant to ask Vaughn about Haskell's nasty remark.

"But not everyone is prejudiced," Betsey said. "I'm certainly not."

"That's true," Joe said. "But where Vaughn is from—Nebraska—many people in his area were prejudiced. Even out here in Wylder, not everyone is accepting. There are a few people, for instance, who want furniture made by me or Henry but not him. Ignorant fools," he finished. "He's an excellent carpenter."

"Well, I'm not that way," Betsey stated. "I may be from back East, and from a fairly wealthy family, but I judge people on their characters, not their background."

"Good for you," Joe said. "I think things are starting to change out here in the West and will eventually, all over. If anyone can convince him, I'm sure you can, Cousin. I know Vaughn well, and you couldn't ask for a more loyal and honest business partner and friend. "

"He should trust me," Betsey insisted.

"Talk to him," Joe urged.

****

She had no chance to talk to Vaughn alone that evening.

Their trip the following day was quiet. They pulled into Wylder early the next afternoon, dusty and mostly happy.

They left the horses and mules at the stable, where Betsey was sure the animals were relieved to also be back in their usual surroundings with their plentiful hay and oats. Then Vaughn and Joe immediately took Louisa to the sheriff, dropping their belongings on the way at the shop. The next priority, Betsey knew, was that the two intended to go to the claim office and officially stake their claim.

One of the stable boys helped Betsey and Nina with their belongings to the hotel. Once she and Nina had enjoyed baths drawn by the hotel's staff, Nina helped Betsey to unpack. She made notes about the whole trip, adding them to her séance notes. Then she even made a few notes about places she might want to sketch from memory for her future paintings. Finally, by five o'clock, she and Nina were organized and ready for a normal meal. But Betsey also felt drained.

They went round to the cabinetry shoppe. She was hoping Joe and Vaughn could join them for supper. And celebrate their discovery of the treasure.

The shop was busy. Several customers were waiting for Joe and Vaughn, while two others were describing custom orders they wanted. Finally, some twenty minutes later, the customers were gone, and Henry and his son were taking their leave.

"We've caught up with Henry, finding out what

work has to be done during the next week," Joe told them. "Now we will prepare for our trip back. There's more men to hire and equipment to buy."

"When are you going back?" Betsey asked. Vaughn stood beside a pile of pick axes and other equipment in the corner of the shop.

"We head out the morning after tomorrow," Joe said.

She felt a pang of disappointment. "So soon?" But she'd known they wouldn't want to wait long, so she was unsurprised. Just disappointed.

"Yup."

"Don't you have time for dinner?" she asked anxiously.

"I'll check with Vaughn. Maybe we can eat quickly and have a drink to celebrate."

****

It had been a nice supper, Vaughn reflected as he and Joe finally were able to get ready for bed. Good food, that someone else cooked, and beer—they'd raised their drinks in a toast to first all of them, then a special one to Betsey. She'd saved them all.

Watching her flush with pleasure, he'd seen how modest she was. "I only did what I had to do," she'd said in a low voice.

Vaughn suspected it wouldn't be long 'til the tale of Haskell's treachery and death, and Louisa's arrest, made its way through the gossips in town. Already, the newspaper editor had stopped into the shop and said he wanted to interview them.

When he and Joe finished dinner quickly, they'd paid and hurried back to the shop, where they'd finished assessing what orders had come in. The shop was growing—they were successful without even considering their exciting find.

Joe had also wasted no time before dinner and went to see Millie, only to learn from the housekeeper that her family was in Cheyenne visiting cousins. They would be away for a week.

He told Vaughn he'd left her a note, saying he had good news. She'd learn from the gossips in town soon enough that they had found Carlos Ayala's mine.

After he said goodnight to his friend, Vaughn found himself too alert to sleep. He had things to do in the morning—finishing getting ready for their next trek into the foothills of the mountains, hiring more people including a bounty hunter they knew who'd be glad to earn some cash to watch their backs.

He had been pacing only for a few minutes when Joe came into their small parlor.

"Can't sleep, either?" he asked his friend.

"No. I'm too excited and also thinking of what this will mean to Millie and me. It can change our lives." Joe paused in speaking and rubbed his hands together. "Have you thought of all this and the impact it will have on you, Vaughn?"

"Well, we'll be busy with our shop. And now, we'll have to hire people to aid us in managing the mine and establishing the museum in Carlos's name," he said. "We'll be so busy."

"But we'll have the ability to hire others to do much of the work," Joe pointed out. "This will change the way we live. I'll be a married man." He sounded almost in awe. "It means you can wed, too, Vaughn." Joe plopped on the sofa.

"Do you think so?" Vaughn asked the question

casually, but he felt his body tense.

"Yes. People here already like and respect you. Now, they'll really look up to you."

"Including Betsey?"

"Vaughn, you don't give her enough credit. She already liked and respected you, before our discovery."

Vaughn dropped to the sofa to sit beside his friend. "I know I'm a half-breed. Nothing can change that."

"But she doesn't care!" Joe declared. "I think you love her, and I believe she feels the same. Her family is not like Millie's. They will accept you for the man you are," he said it with extra emphasis. "Why don't you tell her how you feel? Besides," he added, leaning forward, "I'm the nearest thing she has to a living male relative hereabouts, and I would approve your courting her."

****

Betsey knew Joe had planned to send a telegram this morning to Violet and Drew, simply saying they'd had a successful trip. Betsey wanted to follow up with a telegram of her own. Nina, of course, tagged along, and while Betsey spoke to old Sid, Nina had a few minutes to step outside with Billy.

Betsey's telegram said simply: *Was able to help Joe and Vaughn accomplish their goal. STOP Will write more later STOP Can't wait to meet baby Charles STOP*

After sending the telegram, she wandered around the stores in town with her maid, simply enjoying the town of Wylder. She realized how much it had grown on her. She would miss it and everyone here when she returned to the East. She enjoyed basking in the camaraderie and good will of the townspeople, who doffed their hats and said hello when passing. New York City was never so friendly.

Since Millie and her family were not around, she had a quiet noon day meal with Nina, then sat and read and wrote a long letter to Violet and Drew. By later afternoon, Betsey grew restless, especially after having such busy days while they were away. She knew Joe and Vaughn were busy preparing to leave very early the following day with their entourage, but she hoped for a few minutes with them, especially Vaughn.

When she went over to the shop, Joe told her Vaughn had gone to the general store to purchase a few more things and do their remaining errands, including a delivery of some bookcases. "We realized there were a few other items we needed," he said in a kind voice. "Betsey, I'm sure he'll stop by to say farewell before we leave."

"Well, goodbye and good luck," she told Joe, then hugged him.

He held on to her for a few extra seconds. "For what it's worth, Betsey, we are so grateful to you for what you did. Haskell would have killed us all without hesitation."

"I know," she said into his shoulder. "Joe, something else—I know Nina is my maid, but I feel she's entitled to something for coming with us on this adventure, braving danger, and helping us. She didn't even complain."

"I know, and Vaughn and I discussed what would be fair already," Joe said. "The first few days of mining, we're going to share our finds with you girls—we'll divide the gold up four ways. We want you to get a share, too, Betsey."

"Me? But I don't need the money." she protested. "I am grateful to you, but you share the first find with Nina and then divide it up between you and the men who are working the operation or whatever you think is fair. I could help work on the museum. It would give me a project to do, especially when I go home. I have discovered I like having a purpose, something besides looking at fashions and going to balls and fetes."

Joe squeezed her one more time. "You are a good woman, Betsey Chalmers. You have been an enormous help."

The lump in her throat that formed at his words grew bigger. She swallowed and blinked back sudden tears.

After a dinner spent with Nina, she went back to her room to read, leaving Nina to go in search of her friend Jeannie to chat. Betsey felt kind of at a loss. She'd accomplished what she came for. She supposed on the morrow she'd have to start making plans to return home.

Perhaps, she thought, she'd first do a few more days of painting, while some of the sights she'd seen on their excursion were still fresh in her mind.

Why did she find the idea of returning to New York City so depressing?

She opened her romance novel but was having trouble concentrating. Vaughn's face kept appearing in her mind as he looked when he'd kissed her. His fingers tilting her head up, how soft his lips felt when he started kissing her, then the growing pressure as he kissed her harder…

"Miss Betsey?" Nina interrupted her reverie. She'd taken to speaking to her more formally again, now that they weren't on their trip to the mountains.

"Yes?" Betsey took in the fact that her maid was breathing hard. She must have rushed up the stairs to their rooms. "Is everything all right?

"Oh yes, Miss Betsey. Vaughn—Mr. Montgomery—is here and wants to see you."

Vaughn was here! He did want to say goodbye to her.

Betsey sprang up. "Of course I want to wish him well." She paused to run her brush through her hair, then glanced in the mirror. No time to primp. She wanted to see the man she loved and wish him a successful journey.

She hurried down the stairs. Vaughn was sitting on a nearby sofa. She noted he'd had a recent haircut and shave. He must have done so today, she surmised. He also had on a freshly pressed shirt and looked extra tidy. He stood immediately.

"Betsey," he said in a strangely formal tone, "would you care to take an evening walk outside with me?"

"I'd be delighted," she replied, sliding her hand into the crook of his arm.

They walked outside the hotel and along the boardwalk. He steered them towards the grassy area at the end of the street as dusk was falling.

She wanted to fill the silence. "The colors out here are so beautiful, especially the sunrises and sunsets. I want to do more painting."

"You will enjoy that, I'm sure." He stopped as they stepped off the boardwalk into the grassy area. "Betsey, I'm leaving very early in the morning."

"I know. I-I will miss you both," she admitted.

"Will you? Will you miss me? Or just Joe?"

What was he getting at? "Yes, I will miss you, Vaughn." She took a breath and decided to lay her heart on the line. "I have grown...quite fond of you, Vaughn." Her heart was beating erratically.

"As I have of you, Betsey," he said the words hesitatingly, as if someone was pulling them out. "For the first time in my life, I have—fallen for a woman. For you, Betsey Chalmers." His eyes met hers, unwavering.

Her heart stopped. Vaughn was admitting he had feelings for her!

"Oh, Vaughn," she breathed, barely above a whisper, "I have—I have fallen in love with you."

"You have?" His mouth dropped open. Then his surprised expression was replaced by the widest smile she had ever seen on his face. "I love you, too. I tried to fight it—but I can't. I love you, Betsey." He brought her hands to his lips and kissed them gently.

Her heart was beating like a drum. She stood on tiptoes and putting her hands around his neck, brought his head down to hers, and kissed him.

He responded by pulling her into his arms and kissing her, hard. His lips pressed against hers, and it was as if sunshine burst in her body. She felt light, as if floating away on the spring wind.

"You silly man," she finally gasped out when he loosened his grip, "Why did you ever think I wouldn't love you? You are the best man I've ever met. Loyal and brave and honest."

"But I am a half-breed," he said. "Most women wouldn't want to—have a relationship with a man such as me."

"I'm not most women."

"That's true. You are one in a million. I love you, Betsey." He stroked her cheek. His touch sent thrills all over her body.

"I love you, Vaughn." They stared for a long minute into each other's eyes.

"Then—you'll wait for me?" he asked quietly.

"For you to come back from your journey? Of course, I'll be here waiting."

"Yes. I already spoke to Joe since he's your nearest living male family member around here. He gave me permission to court you."

Betsey sucked in her breath loudly. She knew what he was asking.

"I'll wait for you."

He scooped her up in his arms again. "Yipee!"

Epilogue

"Wylder , next stop!" the conductor called.

Betsey prepared to disembark from the train with her husband. Vaughn gathered their suitcases while she grabbed her carpet bag. The trip east had been a fun one, seeing parts of the country with Vaughn at her side to point out things of interest, visiting her family, and meeting her new cousin while they all got to meet Vaughn.

He'd been pleasantly surprised that her brothers, and Drew and Violet, had been so warm and welcoming to him, she knew. And she'd been doubly grateful for their caring and acceptance. It had been a delightful, if short, visit. They were both anxious to get back to Wylder—Vaughn so he could personally handle things at the shoppe and mine—Betsey because she, quite simply, missed the town that had become her home. While away, she had found herself longing for the slower pace, the beauty of the wide open spaces in this part of the country, and the friends she'd made.

And now, it would be Joe and Millie's turn to travel east so they could visit with Joe's family.

It had been six months since the discovery of the Spaniard's treasure. Vaughn and Betsey had married six weeks after that splendid day, and Joe and Millie a month later. Millie's family had indeed relented in their view of Joe. Although Betsey didn't care for their uppity ways, she was glad Millie and Joe had found happiness, and Betsey was especially happy to have Millie as her friend.

The mine was going well, and she was spearheading the plans for the museum. They had also made a very generous donation to the monastery's orphanage, which Carlos Ayala had been so fond of. Since many of the children there were Indian, Vaughn had been especially proud to make this donation.

Now that they were coming home to Wylder, Vaughn and Betsey planned to build a home on the outskirts of town, next to the one Joe and Millie had already started to build. They would need more space soon—Betsey had a secret she hadn't yet shared with Vaughn. She had realized just before they departed New York that she was increasing. She was so happy and knew Vaughn would be, too.

The biggest surprise came from Nina. They had offered to escort Nina back home to New York. But she had declined.

"Billy and I are making plans," she said proudly. "I like it here, and out in Wyoming, we can have a good future. Billy will be taking over for Old Sid at the telegraph office soon, and he wants to marry me."

She'd been so happy for Nina and understood exactly how she felt.

Vaughn led the way now to the exit as the train pulled into Wylder.

"I can't wait to see everyone and be home!" Betsey declared.

Vaughn sent her a charming grin. She knew he was ecstatic that she liked it here.

"Wylder, Wyoming!" the conductor shouted as the train slowed to a stop. They stepped from the train.

Vaughn turned to help Betsey step down after handing their things to a porter.

Home. Betsey blinked the sudden tears away. Wylder had truly become her home. She loved everything about the town.

Most of all, she loved Vaughn and their life together,

He turned to her, smiling. "Glad to be home, Mrs. Montgomery?"

"Very glad." Her eyes met his, and she winked.

He winked back, and she felt the slow curling of warmth he always caused in her body.

"Vaughn! Betsey!" Joe exclaimed from down the platform. He pushed through the crowd. "Did you have a good trip?"

Betsey was happy to see Millie had accompanied him. "It was wonderful. Now, it's your turn to get away." She hugged her friend.

"We're looking forward to it," Millie declared. "We'll leave next week after the men have had a chance to catch up with things."

"Everything's going well," Joe added.

With business at the cabinetry shoppe booming, and the mine producing a steady stream of gold, they were all amazingly comfortable. And being in Vaughn's arms every night was the best part of it all, Betsey felt.

She turned to him now and threw her arms around him.

"We're home, Vaughn! To stay! I couldn't be happier."

He kissed her soundly. "Me too," he responded. "Me, too, my love."

A word about the author...

Roni Denholtz is the award winning author of 24 romance novels and novellas, including contemporary, historical, paranormal and holiday stories. She lives in beautiful northwest New Jersey with her husband and rescue dog. Her children are grown, and she is now a proud grandmother. She has volunteered for school organizations and pet shelters, and for New Jersey Romance Writers, where she served as president in 2016.

Thank you for purchasing
this publication of The Wild Rose Press, Inc.

For questions or more information
contact us at
info@thewildrosepress.com.

The Wild Rose Press, Inc.
www.thewildrosepress.com